BLACK LACE AND PROMISES

VOLUME 2

FENELLA ASHWORTH

© COPYRIGHT FENELLA ASHWORTH 2021

A NOTE FROM THE AUTHOR

This book contains sex scenes. **Plenty of them.** So if that is likely to upset you, this is probably not the book for you. It might be better to part company now, before my overactive imagination offends you.

But, to the rest of you, welcome!

I'm delighted you have selected this book to read and I really hope you enjoy it.

Enjoy, Fenella x

THIS BOOK IS a work of fiction. Names, characters, places, and incidents are either products of the author's imagination or are used fictitiously. Any resemblance to actual people, living or dead, is entirely coincidental. If you think you recognise one of the characters in this book then congratulations - your friends and family are *waaaaay* more exciting than mine. Please introduce me some time!

All rights reserved. No part of this book may be reproduced in any form or by any electronic or mechanical means including information storage and retrieval systems, without permission in writing from the publisher. The only exception is by a reviewer, who may quote short excerpts in a review.

Please note the spelling throughout is British English.

Thank you for your support.

www.fenellaashworth.com

Copyright © 2022 by Fenella Ashworth

ALSO BY FENELLA ASHWORTH

All books are available on Amazon and KU. Most also have paperback and large print versions. There are also a handful of audiobooks available.

www.fenellaashworth.com

ENGLISH BAD BOYS SERIES

Standalone reads where the wicked desires of sexually experienced men take centre stage

Fictional Fantasies Exxxtended

One Hot Wynter's Night

Right Hand Man

Experimental Pleasures

RESISTANCE IS FUTILE SERIES

Standalone reads where powerful attraction leaves the couple ultimately unable to resist

Animal Attraction

Better Fate Than Never

I Put a Spell on You

Highland Games

REVERSE HAREM - #WHYCHOOSE

Linked reverse harem reads, containing several men and one lucky woman

Three Times Moor Pleasure

Too Much Pleasure

SUGAR & SPICE SERIES

Standalone reads stories of confident alpha men and inexperienced women

Educating Daisy

Patients is a Virtue

Just Another Winter's Tale

THE CRANWORTH CHRONICLES

A linked series based on an arranged marriage with a twist!

To Love, Honour and Oh Pay - Book 1

To Love, Honour and Oh Pay - Book 2

To Love, Honour and Oh Pay - Book 3

DANIEL LAWSON SERIES

A linked series, charting the life of British equestrian Daniel Lawson and his friends

First Love, Second Chance (Book 1)

Perfect Stranger, Strangely Perfect (Book 2)

Feels Just Like Starting Over (Book 3)

No Rain, No Flowers (Book 4)

Easy Come, Easy Go (Book 5)

Darkest Night, Brightest Stars (Book 6)

The Early Years (Book 7)

CANIS HALL SERIES

A linked steamy paranormal romance series, where a woman unknowingly falls for a wolf shifter

Wolf Moon (Book 1)

Hunger Moon (Book 2)

Milk Moon (Book 3)

Pink Moon (Book 4)

Flower Moon (Book 5)

Honey Moon (Book 6)

Thunder Moon (Book 7)

Grain Moon (Book 8)

Harvest Moon (Book 9)

Hunter's Moon (Book 10)

Frost Moon (Book 11)

Cold Moon (Book 12)

FORBIDDEN DESIRES

Standalone reads where forbidden relationships inevitably develop

Management Skills

An Accidental Affair?

Virtually Lovers

Bad Boys go to Heaven

VILLAGE AFFAIRS

A linked series based on the residents of an English village which is far from sleepy

A Very Rural Affair – Book 1

A Very Rural Affair – Book 2

A Very Rural Affair - Book 3

SHORT STORY COMPILATIONS

Compilations of steamy novellas for your reading pleasure.

Black Lace & Promises – Volume 1

Black Lace & Promises – Volume 2

Black Lace & Promises – Volume 3

Black Lace & Promises - Volume 4

Time for a Quick One?

Date 38

SMUT ONLY

Written under the pen name Olivia Harding, these are sets of short stories which are heavy on the smut and lighter on the plot!

Sexy Reads: Age Gap

Sexy Reads: Seductive Cops

ROMANCE ONLY

Written under the pen name Sarah Fennel. Unlike all the other books listed, these have no explicit sex scenes

Difficult to Reach

Difficult to Leave

Just Jump!

Walking Out

Trot On!

THE STORIES IN THIS BOOK

This book contains the following three shorter stories:
1) Kiss of Life
2) Blast from the Past
3) Three Date Rule

Kiss of Life

It was just another ordinary day when Annabel entered the cool, crystal waters for her dawn swim on a deserted stretch of beach in beautiful Devon. Surprised to see a lone surfer attempting to ride the waves into the dangerous bay, Annabel watches in horror as he tumbles into the water, knocking himself unconscious. Having dragged him from the waters, she attempts to resuscitate Leo. Little did she know at the time, although she might have performed the kiss of life on him that day, it is the astonishingly sexy Leo who ultimately breathes life back into her.

Blast from the Past

Well before he was famous, Toby Jacobs had always been hot. Even when Jane shouldn't have been secretly lusting after her brother's best mate, it was an undeniable truth. Happily, Jane had done well to keep her feelings under wraps over the years, meaning that Toby remained oblivious to her lustful imaginings.

That is, until their paths cross on a television dating show and the façade that Jane has been carefully fostering over the decades, comes crashing down around her ears. And that's when she discovers that Toby is way sexier than even her imagination had dared to dream.

Three Date Rule

While out walking her dog on a dark, spooky night in the neighbouring countryside, Rose trips over and knocks her head. Her rescuer appears in the form of James Stirling and, despite the fact they can't make out each other's features in the dim light, the attraction between the couple is instant and indisputable. Their attraction only grows with each subsequent meeting, but will they successfully manage to fight off their growing lustful desires once James invokes his three date rule, or will nature take control?

KISS OF LIFE

FENELLA ASHWORTH

CHAPTER 1

ANNABEL

The air is refreshingly cool, crisp and salty and I gratefully consume a huge lungful, while gazing out at the glorious scene before me. Squinting slightly against the rising sun which hangs low in an orange sky, the sparkling sea has rarely looked more beautiful. But I know that this perfect cove, located on a secluded stretch of the Devonshire coastline, with its azure blue skies and even bluer surf, conceals a dangerous truth. Beneath the cliffs, just below the crystal clear waters, sprawl a protrusion of rocks which are lethal to boats, surfers and bathers alike. Fortunately, having swum here for years, I'm well versed in where I can and can't roam.

Glancing quickly around me to ensure nobody is in the vicinity, I hastily remove my T-shirt, shorts and sandals, to reveal my swimsuit beneath. Leaving my clothing folded neatly on the beach, well out of the way of any encroaching surf, I make a dash for the water. I've been self-conscious about my body for my entire life, which explains why you find me and my relatively fat ass in this isolated cove, when there's a far superior location about a mile down the coast. I have christened it Babe Beach because it's brimming with size zero, super-model wannabees. But I could never feel comfortable wearing a swimming costume on *that* beach, under the judging glare of prying eyes. Hell, I don't even feel comfortable in my own shower, but at least at home, I don't also feel observed.

Striding purposefully into the surf, trying to ignore the ice-cold temperature, I realise that one of the few times I feel truly comfortable within myself is when I swim. Hidden beneath the waves, I am free; just me and the raw power of nature. As I submerge my shoulders beneath the frigid surf, I can't actually remember a time when I didn't feel self-conscious about my appearance. At school, I was always slightly heavier than my classmates, although it was never serious enough to be a medical problem...just a psychological one. As a teenager, I recall hearing a well-meaning family friend refer to my build as having *puppy fat*. As much as I'd like to continue using that as a valid excuse, I fear at thirty-four years of age, I'm far from being able to categorise myself as a puppy.

Moving swiftly through the shallows, heading for the slightly deeper water, a reflection catches my eye. Most unusually for this time of the morning, I catch sight of another person moving slowly into view on the seaward side of the cove. Sitting astride a surfboard, legs dangling in the water, he is gazing vacantly into the distance. Just from the outline of his broad shoulders and general build, I can tell it's a man. I glance quickly back to the shore. Should I finish my swim early and return to my car? The reason I travel to this isolated location is because it is *always* deserted, almost without exception. Now aware of another human being nearby, I can sense my level of enjoyment decreasing by the second.

Suddenly, something seems to break his daze and he lays down on the surfboard, paddling out to deeper water. A chill traverses my spine, which has nothing to do with the cold temperature. No doubt unaware of the dangers this cove presents, it looks as though he's going to try and surf this way. It's a very bad idea. I try to shout, desperately waving my arm to warn him, but to no avail. Having waited for the next suitable surge, I see him rise up easily onto his surfboard and ride what is a fairly mediocre wave in my direction. Seconds later, just as he reaches the section of water I know houses a dangerous section of rocks, he disappears from sight.

'Fuck,' I moan, lifting my head as high as the rolling ebb and flow of water surrounding me permits. He doesn't seem to have resurfaced. Instinctively, I head to the spot where I last saw the surfer. I'm a strong swimmer and within no time, manage to spy his surfboard. Attached to the object via a leg rope which is Velcroed around his ankle, is the man's lifeless body. My heartrate instantaneously speeds up as I power the last few meters towards him, no thought given for my own safety in the increasingly rough waters.

For a moment I pause in horror at the scene, only able to feel my heart hammering in my chest cavity, aware that my breathing has become fast and shallow. And then instinct kicks in. Manhandling his torso as best I can towards the surfboard, I manage to get his heavy, powerful arms over the object. His lifeless form and cold, wet skin feel alien beneath my touch, but still I continue. Lining up behind him, I power us both towards the shore, my legs burning with strenuous effort. Aware I'm in the dangerous section of water which I always avoid, I keep going nevertheless. Thanks to the overload of adrenaline currently swamping me, I'm unaware of pain coursing through me, each time I kick my legs and feet against the jagged outcrop of rocks just below the surface.

With a cry of relief, I eventually feel the sand beneath my feet and start to heave us out of the shallows. Thank God. We are nearing dry land. I glance quickly around the beach in the hope of commandeering some help but, as usual, there is no-one. This is something I'll have to handle alone. Unfortunately, as the water becomes increasingly shallow, my ability to move this large man diminishes. I do my best, but I can only get his head up onto the sand. The rest of his cold, limp body remains mostly in the shallows, too physically heavy for me to drag out of the water. It takes all of my remaining strength to roll him onto his back. For the first time in my life, I'm grateful to have a little extra weight behind me, to assist with this. He's still unresponsive and I know that if I don't act swiftly, he could well die. Horrified thoughts fill my mind which I attempt to push away. That can't be allowed to happen; he only looks about my age. I *have* to concentrate. A man's life depends on it.

I learnt CPR at work years ago. And I mean *years* ago, to the point that it is only a vague, dim and distant memory. ABC. That's all I remember. Airway, Breathing, Circulation. His mouth is open and I lean down towards him. He smells good; a very masculine scent with the faint whiff of a deodorant or aftershave that set my senses reeling.

'For fuck's sake, focus! What is wrong with you?' I silently berate myself. 'He won't be smelling so good when he's dead, will he?'

I force my mind back to my CPR training. The classroom was airless, with dust floating languidly through the fingers of sunlight that shone into the stuffy room. It had been a hot, summer's day. Annie, the plastic training head and torso, spent her time lying in the middle of the floor. Each time I'd had to kneel down and lower my mouth to her synthetic one, she'd tasted of bitter, antibacterial wipes. A. Airway. I gaze into his mouth and can't see an obstruction, although I fear his windpipe may well contain seawater. B. Breathing. I realise with horror that he isn't. No rise and fall of his chest is visible, and I can't feel any breath from his mouth. C. Circulation. My fingers scrabble for his wrist, desperate to feel a pulse. I pause, trying hard to concentrate. I think I can feel one, but it's so difficult to tell with the waves lapping around us. I place the heel of my hand firmly over his broad, slightly hairy chest. Yes. Yes, there is definitely a heartbeat. Please God, don't let him die.

Leaning over his face, I try to remember my training. I'm pretty sure the next step is to do five rescue breaths. Lifting up his chin to open his airway and mouth, I place two fingers around his nose and squeeze to prevent any loss of air. Then, taking a deep breath, I lower my mouth to his. His lips are cold, wet and taste strongly of salt. I can feel the faint stubble from his face digging into me. Forming a seal, I breathe strongly. Although not entirely sure, I think his chest rises slightly beside me. Retracting for a moment, I inhale fast and deep, before trying once more, aware that the continuous waves breaking on the beach are hampering my efforts.

'Come on!' I scream at him in despair, after the second rescue breath. I'm surprised to feel angry, as though expecting this stranger to, at least in some way, assist with his own resuscitation. In terrified frustration, I slam my fist down hard against his chest, before returning to my position and administering a third breath. And suddenly, it happens. Amidst a flurry of lurching and choking, he regains consciousness and I help push his head to one side as he regurgitates sea water. Having groggily wiped his mouth with the back of his hand, he gazes up at me with the bluest eyes I have ever seen. Immediately, a spasm of longing makes my abdomen clench violently and unexpectedly. Now I'm the one in danger of drowning.

CHAPTER 2

LEO

I feel weird. Dizzy and disorientated. I remember I'd been watching a lone figure on the distant beach, while I was playing with some song lyrics in my mind that were refusing to take shape. This isn't my local surfing haunt, but I was searching for inspiration, having been under some pressure to write a new song for the band. Due to some copyright issue or other, they've been forced to pull one of the original tracks from their latest album, which is due to be released soon. Consequently, they need a replacement pretty damn fast. Various other songwriters are after the gig, but given I've penned them a number of songs before, the guys kindly approached me first.

Having failed to find the necessary inspiration, I'd picked up a wave and started surfing towards the shore. The mouth to the cove had been narrow, but I've always been up for a challenge. Confusingly, after that, I don't remember anything at all. Except now, I seem to be lying on the sand, next to my board, staring up into the face of a woman I don't recognise. God, I hope I don't have amnesia and ought to know who she is. Well, you hear about that happening, don't you? With long dark hair, freckles across her sweet face and what I sense is a great body, she's certainly the kind of woman I naturally find attractive, so perhaps she's my date? Shading my eyes from the bright sun, I study her carefully.

'You okay?' I ask, making abortive attempts to crawl a little way up the beach, to get out of the surf. I mean, clearly she isn't. Not only is she breathing heavily, with a wild, terrified look in her eyes, but her legs and feet are badly bruised and bleeding.

'Er...yeah,' she replies, looking almost as confused as I feel. 'But we do need to get to a hospital.'

'Why?' I mean, the damage to her legs looks painful, but I'm not convinced it necessitates a hospital visit.

'Because you stopped breathing,' she gabbled. 'And we're completely alone. And I don't have a phone. And it doesn't look like you have a phone. And you need medical attention.'

But all I hear is her first statement.

'I stopped breathing?' I repeat stupidly.

'Yeah,' she nodded, looking strained. 'Look, my car's just there.'

I attempt to gaze in the direction she's pointing, to note a small red vehicle parked alone on the roadside.

'Do you think you can get up the beach?' she asks, making a quick grab for her nearby pile of clothes, before tugging them on unceremoniously. I can tell from her demeanour that she is shy about her appearance, although heaven knows why. Not only is she naturally pretty without requiring a scrap of make-up, but she has the most incredible ass, and legs that go on and on.

'Course,' I reply, unsure why she feels the need to ask. It can't be more than thirty meters away.

Accepting her assistance, I struggle to my feet, trying to ignore the sensation of dizziness which is swooping and swirling through my brain. As I straighten up to my full six foot three in height, I'm aware that I tower somewhat over my companion. Keeping hold of her arm, I stagger forwards, embarrassed to find myself struggling. My muscles feel exhausted and my lungs ache like hell. When did walking suddenly become such hard work? What on earth is wrong with me? I'm normally really fit. I can't deny that I feel a great sense of relief once we reach her car and I collapse into the passenger seat.

Within moments, she's located a fleecy jumper which is undoubtedly extremely baggy on her, but just about fits me. I'm grateful for it, along with the blanket now wrapped around my legs. My body has started to shake, although I'm not sure if that's from the cold or the shock. Maybe she's correct; perhaps we do need to visit the hospital after all.

'You okay?' she asks, looking as concerned as ever.

'Mmmm, great,' I sigh, as we move off down the road. The truth is, I'm feeling surprisingly elated...almost spaced out. 'I might have a little snooze though, if you don't mind?'

'No!' she exclaims with such determination that I almost leap from my chair. 'I'm not risking you falling unconscious on me again!'

Giving myself a mental shake, I open the window wide and allow the cool air to hit me dead in the face. She's right. I'd already seen the expression of fear in her eyes when we were on the beach. I want to avoid her feeling that way again.

'Sorry,' I shrug, making every effort to stay present. 'I'm not much of a date, am I?'

'What's your name?' she asks quickly, avoiding my question extremely effectively. So maybe I shouldn't know who she is, after all.

'Leo. Leo Wilson.' I'm obviously a little slow off the mark to ask hers because she's already powered on with the next question.

'Home Address?'

'Err...' What the fuck is going on here? A job interview? 'Forty-seven, Lime Tree Avenue, Dartmouth. Want my phone number as well?'

'Um, no,' she quickly mutters, a blush spreading across her face and neck which makes her look even cuter.

'So, tell me your name?'

'Annabel Fox.'

'Very nice to meet you. Need to know any other personal information about me, Annabel Fox?' I ask, enjoying the way my tongue wraps around her name. 'Inside leg measurement? Sexual history, perhaps?' She flushes even deeper and I experience a perverse sense of enjoyment, in watching her struggle. Indeed, just interacting with Annabel in this way is already starting to make me feel better.

'Actually, now you mention it, your date of birth would be useful,' she replies unexpectedly and I'm pleased to discover that the kitten has claws.

'Why do you want to know that?'

'Just in case you...fall asleep again,' she admits, clearly choosing her words carefully. But we both know she's preparing for the worst. Should I lose consciousness once more, she'll be required to confirm personal details on my behalf.

'The fifth of September, nineteen eighty-two,' I admit softly. The truth is, I'm grateful to this stranger who has not only helped me out of the water, but continues to look out for my welfare.

'Ah!' she cries, looking relieved. 'That's one day before my mum's birthday. I'll remember that.'

'Your mum's thirty-eight?' I joke, pretending to look impressed. 'What a coincidence!'

'Same day, not same year...as well you know,' she chuckles. I watch her with interest; it's the first time since we've met that I've seen her smile, and in my weakened state, I sense my heart flutter in response.

'When's yours?' She tells me and I quickly do the maths. 'Mmmm, good age difference,' I observe with satisfaction.

'For what?' yelps Annabel, clearly not sure how to handle my directness.

'All sorts,' I grin, amused to see her blush even more furiously.

'The hospital is only a few minutes away now,' she stutters, clearly trying to regain control. We both know she's lying but I let it slide. Reaching out for the stereo, she turns up the volume to fill the provocative silence.

I'm not entirely sure what's wrong with me but all I can think about is sex. It's as though I need to experience something life affirming after my near miss, ideally with this super cute woman. I yearn to feel her soft skin beneath my fingers, her quivering desire beneath my tongue, her arousal on my taste buds and witness a sheer desperation in her eyes. To drive her through the most intense pleasure of her life and feel her come apart in my arms. Sensibly, my thoughts remain unshared and I stay silent, until one of my favourite tracks of all time slinks its way onto the radio.

'Oh God! I love this song!' she exclaims, before I have a chance to react. 'Mind if we turn it up?'

'Not at all,' I enthuse. She's right; it's a cracking tune. I only wish I'd written it myself. I reach forwards to adjust the volume at exactly the same time as she does. In that briefest of moments, our fingers brush. Immediately, she snatches her hand away, as though my skin is searing with heat. At the same time, the previously well-driven car descends into a flurry of judders and jerks. Making no comment, I turn up the volume to just the wrong side of acceptable. Minutes later, we roar into the hospital car park, bellowing out the final chorus at the very tops of our voices. In a strange way, the time I've just spent with Annabel has been equally life affirming as the original, much more racy scenario I had in mind...well, almost.

CHAPTER 3

LEO

I'm sitting beside Annabel in the hospital waiting room, the hard, plastic chair digging uncomfortably into my back. We've managed to drink our way through multiple bottles of water and consume all the aged mints and sweets we could find in her handbag. They've been helping to block out the overpowering smell of cheap disinfectant which pervades the air. The blinds are pulled down on the windows, blocking out all natural light and making it feel like we're trapped in a sealed box. I keep glancing unenthusiastically at the other waiting patients. Normally, I enjoy people-watching but this location is offering extremely slim pickings. Besides, there is only one person that intrigues me in this building, and I can't very well sit and stare at her.

'Leo Wilson?' enquires an authoritative voice from the other side of the room.

Automatically, I stand. Having been out of the sea for nearly three hours now, my skin feels uncomfortable; alien almost. It has dried, salty and tight. I'm desperate to get home and shower. I've had a number of triage nurses visit since we arrived, flicking torch lights in my eyes, checking my pulse, and all manner of other activities, grouped under the guise of *tests*. This is the first time I'll be seen by an actual doctor.

'Yes,' I reply.

'This way, please,' the medic requests, starting to walk in the opposite direction to me. I glance down at Annabel who hasn't moved.

'I'll wait here for you,' she explains, in response to my questioning gaze.

'No, you can't! I need you to come with me. After all, you're the only one that knows what happened. I was out for the count, remember?' I add, with a teasing smile.

Swiftly, we make our way towards the doctor and follow him along a corridor. We are led into a small consultation room, with a random surplus of abandoned medical equipment along the walls and a computer terminal on an otherwise empty desk.

'Would you please explain what happened?' asked the doctor, removing the stethoscope from around his neck before heading in my direction with the resonator poised for action. 'And can you remove your top please?' he adds, as it becomes apparent that Annabel's tightly-fitting fleece is going to prevent the necessary checks from being performed. Without a thought, I pull the garment straight over my head, exposing my chest and back. I'm surprised to sense Annabel, who is sitting beside me, turn her head bashfully away. It isn't like she hasn't seen me in a state of undress before. I'd only been wearing trunks on the beach, after all.

'I was surfing and...that's kind of the last thing I remember,' I joke. 'But hopefully Annabel here can fill in the blanks?'

I turn to my companion who raises her chin and prepares to provide the details I am unaware of.

'The cove Leo surfed into has some dangerously shallow rocks. I guess he hit one, fell and got knocked out. I swam across to him, dragged him onto the surfboard and paddled us both to shore.'

'Does that explain the state of your lower legs?' the doctor queried. 'Speaking of which, I should take a look at your injuries before you leave too.'

Annabel nods in confirmation. Just then, a cold chill runs straight through my spine and I feel my jaw slacken. In my dazed, vacant state, I hadn't appreciated that her beautiful legs had been damaged, in order to rescue me. As though it's the most natural thing on earth, I reach for one of her warm, soft hands, which are clenched tightly in her lap. She stares up at me in disbelief, blushing furiously, and we share a moment.

'I'm so sorry,' I mutter.

'And then?' prompts the doctor at last. Breaking our connection, Annabel forces her gaze from mine but I continue to squeeze her hand. When she returns to her story, her tone is noticeably higher and more strained than before.

'Um...I...managed to get Leo partly out of the water and roll him onto his back. He wasn't breathing but he did have a pulse. There was nobody around to help so I began to...administer the kiss of life.'

It is the most surreal experience, hearing a description of what someone did to my body, when I have absolutely zero knowledge of it taking place. I suddenly start to realise the magnitude of what actually happened today.

'What did you do?'

'I began to give Leo five rescue breaths. He didn't respond after two, so I...er...'

'Yes?' encouraged the doctor, but if he hadn't asked I definitely would have. She looks as guilty as hell.

'I...might have hit his chest in desperation...sorry,' she adds in my general direction, failing to meet my eyes. I can't help but raise a single, amused eyebrow in response to her antics. 'But he came round on the third breath.'

'And approximately how much time elapsed between you seeing Mr Wilson fall, and him regaining consciousness, do you think?'

'Um...I don't know exactly...it was probably only two or three minutes, although it felt like a lot more.'

'I bet,' smiles the doctor in admiration. 'Well, your actions undoubtedly saved a man's life today. And not only that, but the swiftness with which you undertook them prevented him from suffering any permanent damage. Well done.'

'Thank you,' she responds quietly, head bowed down in embarrassment.

'You saved my life?' I query in astonishment. There had been a disconnect in my mind, between the last few hours and reality. However, that connection has been very firmly restored now. I could be dead. That's the message I'm getting loud and clear from the medical staff. And what's more, the woman sitting next to me, in the form of my guardian angel, is the only reason why I'm not. So why is my mind fixated on how sexy my saviour is? She covered herself up quickly on the beach, but not before I'd caught sight of a body I could lose myself in. That's when the power with which I desire this woman unexpectedly hits me like a steam train.

'I just did what anyone would have done,' she blusters.

'You saved my life,' I repeat more firmly. That fact is something which will remain with me, until my dying day. And the impact she is currently having on my mind and body isn't something I'm ever likely to forget either.

CHAPTER 4

ANNABEL

My heart is feeling heavy as I drive the final mile of our journey together. Having left the cove, Leo's surfboard now strapped to the roof, we are heading towards Babe Beach to collect his car. After that...who knows? But I shall be sorry to say goodbye to this man with whom I feel I have a close connection. As though wanting to confirm he's still beside me, I glance across at the passenger seat to be confronted by a thick, muscled pair of thighs visible from beneath his shorts which have long since dried. Straightaway, I wish I hadn't done so. Fuck, he has an amazing body! I quickly return my eyes to the road, before my gaze has reached anywhere near his face.

'You okay?' he queries, looking across. Given my now flustered disposition, along with the erratic progress the car is making, it isn't difficult to imagine that something has rattled me.

'Fine,' I gasp, desperately trying to keep my mind away from the subject of just how damn hot my passenger is...and how horrendously sexually frustrated I feel.

'If you take a left here,' he advises, raising his hand to point towards the main road that runs along the wide stretch of sand, my car's that dark green one.

I follow his instructions. Parking, I switch off the engine and scurry outside to assist with his surfboard, before he has a chance to engage me in any further conversation. Immediately, I feel self-conscious. All around us are body-beautiful women, displaying all their wares to full effect. I couldn't compete with them in a million years and, in all honesty, I wouldn't want to try. Exposing my curves to random strangers simply isn't in my nature.

As it happens, I'm probably not as unattractive as I think, situated somewhere on the sliding scale between anorexic and requiring a crane to leave the house. I remember in my twenties, having a similarly low opinion of myself; never looking in the mirror, always covering up. I was undeniably heavier than I wanted to be back then. But now, if I look back at photographs of myself from that time, I'm surprised to find I don't look *that* bad. I mean, I do have a huge ass, compared to the stick insects currently flitting around us, not very subtly giving Leo the eye. But some men like that, right? Suddenly, all my self-indulgent thoughts are wiped clean from my mind. Having secured the surfboard to the roof of his vehicle, Leo has returned to me and quite unexpectedly trapped me against my car with his own, incredible physique.

'What are you doing?' I gasp, astounded to find myself in this position, in front of the entire beach. Through my soft fleece that he continues to wear, I can feel the hardness of his body pressing into my own. The scent of him is almost overwhelming and the soft caress of his breath against my cheek is making me feel dizzy with lust.

'I'm not letting you escape until you promise to go out with me.'

My hands are hanging loosely by my sides, until he starts to entwine his fingers with mine. I'm astonished to find myself returning the pressure, encouraging him on against my will.

'You mean for lunch?' I stutter, my brain no longer fully functioning. 'I'm not hungry.' For some reason, Leo seems to find this amusing.

'No, me neither,' he confirms, his beautiful mouth curling into a twisted smile. 'Strange, that.' What the hell does that mean? There is some serious subtext going on here which I haven't yet grasped.

'Go out on a date with me,' he clarifies. I glance up at him, trying not to be overwhelmed by his great looming presence. As our eyes lock, a heat blisters through my abdomen, engaging every synapse in my brain and making me feel more alive than I have ever known.

'That's really not necessary,' I reply breathlessly.

'I beg to differ,' is his only response.

'I'll...go out with you as a friend,' I manage to croak. It feels as though he's devouring me with his eyes. My throat is dry, my legs heavy and weak...I can scarcely breathe.

'Oh God! Are you in a relationship?' he asks, looking guilty as he draws back very slightly. I see his eyes flicker down to my left hand, as though to check I'm not wearing a ring.

'I'm not sure how that's relevant, but no,' I reply, bristling slightly. 'I'm single.' And I can scarcely remember a time when I wasn't, I don't add out loud.

He nods and with a smile, leans back against me.

'Why is that funny?' I demand, somehow finding the strength to argue, despite the way he's making me feel.

'Not funny. Exhilarating.'

'Why?'

'Because it allows me to ask my next question,' he admits with a grin.

'Which is?' I whisper. In all honesty, I'm not sure I want to know, but some kind of perverse instinct is forcing me to continually engage.

'Will you kiss me?'

'On your cheek?' I ask quietly, glancing around quickly, concerned that people might be watching us. I'm aware of heat rushing to my face as I watch Leo slowly shake his head in answer to my question.

'No. Full on my mouth.' He must have read my answer through my silent, shocked response. 'Right here,' he continued, ramping up the anticipation to a point I can no longer bear. 'Right now.'

'I...um...no...well...can't.'

'Why not?' he mutters in a low sexy tone. 'You've already kissed me once. This time, I'd like to be awake to enjoy the experience.'

'That is *entirely* different and you know it!' I exclaim, a fighting spirit knocking me straight out of the shyness which was threatening to engulf me.

'Perhaps,' he shrugs with a grin.

'Why would you even want me to?' I don't understand what game he's playing, but given the experience we've gone through today, I don't think it's a very fair one.

'That is a *very* strange thing to ask. I'd have thought my reasoning was blatantly obvious.' He must have empathised with something in my confused demeanour, for the next time he spoke, it was in a gentler, yet no less firm tone.

'Either kiss me right now, or go on a *proper* date with me tomorrow night.' It was a final ultimatum. I'm not convinced I have a lot of choice, although deep down inside, it doesn't matter. I know exactly how desperate I am to see this incredible man again.

'Okay,' I agree breathily. 'A date.'

For a precious moment, all time stands still as he drops down even closer to my face and stares me dead in the eyes.

'Promise me,' he says seriously.

'I promise.'

'In which case, I'll pick you up from home at six o'clock,' he explains, obviously in no rush to release me. I can feel his breath ghosting across my cheek now, the scent of him filling my lungs and making me quite dizzy with need. His lips are mere centimetres away from mine. Why isn't he moving away?

'Okay,' I croak, utterly overwhelmed by his nearness. 'But you don't know my address.'

'Seashell cottage, Frogmore, right? You provided it to the hospital staff.'

'How on earth do you remember that?'

'Let's just say, you've made quite an impression on me,' he admits quietly, before lowering his mouth towards mine. Time stops. I can sense the solid beat of my heart thundering around my body. The rush of the waves. The caress of the sea breeze. And him. All other things cease to exist. Just him. Only him.

The very lightest brush of his lips against mine provides the most chaste, gentle kiss I have ever known...almost barely there. But that briefest touch was accompanied by the taste of promise, lust and passion, the kind of which I have never before imagined, let alone experienced. With a low groan, he slides his mouth towards my ear. My body automatically reacts, without permission from my conscious mind. Arching my neck away to provide Leo with easier access, I groan deep down in my throat. I sound hungry, hedonistic and nothing like the way I normally act.

'Mmmmm,' he moans in my ear. The sound causes every hair on the back of my neck to stand to attention, as goosebumps flood across my arms and chest. 'Walking away from you right now is going to be the hardest thing I've ever done. But I'm going to do it all the same, for both of our sake's. I'll see you tomorrow evening.'

And with that, he takes one purposeful step back, sends me a brief smile, clambers into his car and roars away. Minutes after Leo has gone, I can still be found in exactly the same position in which he left me, collapsed against the side of my car. Both my mouth and eyes remain wide open in shock as I try to both savour and process what on earth happened. I might have made an impression on him, but I'm willing to bet, it is *nothing* like the impression he's just made on me.

CHAPTER 5

ANNABEL

I'm amazed at how quickly one day can pass. It feels like moments ago I was standing beside Leo, agreeing to go on a date with him, and now here we are. In only a matter of hours, he'll be picking me up and I am swamped by the indecision of what to wear. Fleetingly, I flirt with the idea of popping to the shops to purchase something new, but in my heart I know that will be too stressful. Nothing ever seems to fit properly. Trousers are invariably too tight around the ass and thighs and too loose around the waist. Sleeves always feel too tight around my arms, yet I feel obliged to wear long sleeves, in order to hide as much of my body from public view as possible. It's an impossible Catch 22 situation which I've existed in for my entire life, so I'm hardly going to resolve it before our date tonight.

Thanks to my mind being in a confused blur, with no idea what to wear, how to feel or what to think, I find myself unable to focus on even the smallest task. Maybe I'll just go with my standard fall back at any social occasion. With a nipped in waist, my black trouser suit hides a multitude of sins. Fortunately, I am disturbed by my beeping phone, signifying an incoming text. It's from the man himself.

"Can't wait to see you x"

Instantly, my tummy rolls with apprehension and I am treated to a massive shot of adrenaline, which as good as floors me. How the hell am I going to survive the rest of today if that is the effect he has on me from miles away? Pushing aside my general feelings of angst, I reply.

"I can't wait either. Where are we going?"

"It's a surprise." His text is more than a little unhelpful. I know it makes me look completely amateurish, asking my date what I should wear, but I do it all the same. I don't mind admitting I'm an amateur, compared to him.

"Please can you give me a clue? I have absolutely no idea what to wear." I can almost imagine him laughing at his screen, shaking his head in disbelief at my total incompetence. Then I speak sternly to myself. I mustn't compare myself to others; Leo chose to go out on a date with me. His responding text surprises me, being both empathetic and helpful.

"If I were you, knowing what I do about the chosen venue, I'd go for jeans, boots, a top and jacket. Does that help?"

I breathe a huge sigh of relief.

"More than you know. Thank you so much." I immediately press send and then wish I hadn't; there is no doubt my level of desperation shines through in that message. I throw the phone down on my bed and start to busy myself, tidying up the wardrobe and selecting my clothing for the evening, for now everything is very clear in my mind. I know exactly what I'll be wearing. Only after I'm ready do I notice that Leo sent me a reply some while previously.

"TBH I don't care what you're wearing. I just can't wait to spend some more time with you."

As promised, Leo arrives very punctually that evening. Kissing me gently, yet very properly on my cheek, he takes my hand and leads me towards his car. It is quite different to the vehicle we attached his surfboard to the previous day; low, open-topped and immaculately maintained, his car is more a work of art than a method of transport.

'Wow, this is gorgeous,' I breathe, as we whizz past the greenest pastures and hedgerows, all bathed in the rich orange, evening sunlight. I've always admired classic cars; not surprising really, given my dad has owned his pride and joy since I was old enough to walk.

'Thank you,' he smiles, looking genuinely pleased with my response.

Soon, we are on the outskirts of the nearby city of Exeter, the stereo blasting out hit after hit, making our journey a fun-filled one with plenty of hysterical singing. It's a real thrill to find a guy I just click with, so completely. The closer we travel to the centre, the more obvious it becomes that there is a significant event taking place there that evening. And suddenly, I remember. A well-known local band, one of my favourites as it happens, has recently broken the international market and are celebrating by playing a huge stadium gig to their home supporters. As the flow of cars slows substantially, I wonder if Leo wishes he'd chosen a restaurant in another location.

'There's a lot of traffic,' I observe, as we grind to a halt.

'Yeah, can't be helped,' he shrugs. 'But it's no problem. We'll be past all this in a moment. Our turning is just here.'

As we slowly edge forwards, Leo turns up a one-way lane labelled 'VIP's Only'. With confusion, I glance around me. Surely, we aren't going to the concert are we? I remember this event being mentioned on the radio the other day. The local area was being advised to brace itself for a certain level of disruption. I know for a fact that tickets have been sold out for months. There is no way he could have obtained entry passes in the past twenty-four hours.

In excited silence, I watch as Leo is guided into a security-checked area. Having shown them a card which I fail to catch sight of properly, we are directed into a covered car park, protected by barriers and security guards, alongside a range of cars even more exquisite than the one I have the honour of sitting in.

'Um...are we...?'

'Let's go,' he grins, failing to respond to my babbling, non-entity of a question. Jumping out of the car, he opens my door and offers a hand to assist me out. His skin feels soft and warm. It immediately sends a zing along my arm that I can't fail to ignore. We make our way towards a guarded doorway. Once again, Leo flashes a card and we are permitted entry.

'Hey! How ya doing, mate?' calls a voice, as we stroll down a plush hallway.

'Stevie!' exclaims Leo, throwing his arm around a man who looks more than a little familiar. Abruptly, my jaw drops wide open in shock. He's the drummer of the main act playing here tonight. I scarcely hear Leo's next words as he flashes a cheeky grin in my direction. 'May I introduce Annabel? She's my date; the woman I was telling you about.'

'In that case, I'm very honoured to meet you,' beamed Stevie. In disbelief, I watch as my hand is scooped up by this rock legend, gently kissed and then lowered back down again. 'I've got to go and warm up, but I really hope to catch up with you later?'

'Sure,' I just about manage to croak, as one of my heroes lopes away. 'Acquaintance of yours?' I ask in utter shock. Yet somewhere in my consciousness, I'm warmed by the knowledge that Leo has spoken about me to one of his friends.

'Something like that,' he shrugs modestly, before leading me onwards once more.

'You've got to give me more than that!' I complain. It's obvious he's hiding something and I've never been great at being kept out of the loop.

'You're bossy,' observes Leo, flashing me a cheeky grin.

'Assertive,' I correct, standing my ground.

'Is that what we're calling it?'

'Yeah, that's what we're calling it,' I giggle. 'So?'

'I'm a songwriter,' he admits at last. 'And I've been lucky enough to work with these guys on a few of their numbers.'

'Seriously?' I couldn't be more impressed. 'Which ones?'

'That's for me to know and you to guess,' he teases. 'This is us.'

I am led into an exquisitely presented room, thronging with noisy guests. Around the perimeter, large tables covered in white linen cloths and decorated with beautiful bold flower displays, are brimming over with mouth-watering food. Meanwhile, waiters dressed in black suits and bow ties, calmly offer up all manner of beverages and canapes. All along the far side of the room is a huge, floor to ceiling window, leading out to a balcony. As we head in that direction, I can see we have the most amazing view of the stage below.

'This is too much,' I breathe, as Leo procures a couple of glasses of expensive champagne and offers one to me. Nervously, I take a large gulp, trying not to cough as the bubbles tickle my nose. Somewhere outside, I hear the first few chords from the warm-up band and a huge cheer echoes around the arena below us.

'This is nothing,' he shrugs. 'In fact, given I get complimentary entry to the event, it actually makes me an incredible cheapskate to bring you here. I'll have to make up for it later...'

I have no idea what that statement means, but my body seems to know. Reacting outside of my control, my legs have gone shaky once more. My tummy feels as though I've just descended a staircase and missed the bottom flight of steps.

'You don't need to do that...' I stutter.

'Oh?' he grins, leaning in close. 'In that case, you can make it up to me.'

'How?'

'Well, you might remember there is something I need from you?' Gazing directly into his wickedly blue eyes, I think I might just faint. A massive surge of heat floods me. I'm not sure I've ever felt lust like this. I'm utterly overwhelmed and yet, as he continues to talk, I'm unable to break our connection. 'Just to give you a heads-up, I'll be requesting that kiss you owe me later tonight.'

CHAPTER 6

LEO

I can't believe how much of a good time I'm having here with Annabel. She's so easy to get along with and yet, at the same time, she provides me with a challenge. She's funny, sexy and assertive, yet whenever I teasingly come onto her, she turns really shy. It's the most endearing paradox. I simply can't get enough of her. I urgently want to reach out, hold her against me and never let go. Equally, I don't want to scare her away and I'm aware that one false move has the potential to screw things up.

Hanging over the balcony, we are both roaring with the rest of the crowd as one of the guys' most famous anthems is belted at high volume across the stadium. Suddenly, she turns to face me.

'This is one of yours, isn't it?' she demands. 'I'm starting to recognise your style.'

With a small smile, I nod. Seeing tens of thousands of people singing the lyrics to a song I have written is certainly not an experience I'll ever truly get used to. But it's incredible to have someone to share it with.

'You're amazing!' she mouths, shaking her head at me in awe. I swallow hard, as a cold prickle of realisation traverses my spine. I really like this girl. Really, *really* like. Her focus has already returned to the stage, but I can't tear my eyes away from her. And then it happens; the inspiration I was searching for in the cove the previous day hits me with full force. My mind starts toying with lyrics which fit the melody that's been circling my mind for weeks; breathing life into this weary heart, you've made me live again. Urgently, I tap Annabel on the arm.

'Do you have a pen and paper in your bag?'

'Sure,' she smiles, looking slightly confused. Having dug around in her handbag, she locates the items and passes them across. Immediately, I start scribbling, desperate to capture the ideas which are free-flowing once more. Appreciating that I need a moment, Annabel returns her attention to the stage, allowing me a number of opportunities to admire her without observation. Just being near her does something magical to me, including allowing the previously caged lyrics to escape from my very soul.

On the pretext of returning her notepad and pen, I shuffle up close beside her while a love ballad is being played on stage. The stadium lights have been dimmed and fifty thousand people are chanting along with the melody, holding lighters and phones in the air. The sight is slightly eerie but strangely inspiring.

'Go out with me again tomorrow?' I mutter, placing my hand over one of hers. Annabel turns to look at me and I think I catch sight of confusion, mixed with a little sorrow.

'I'm not looking for a relationship,' she explains so quietly, that I have to bend in even closer to hear her. 'After a run of bad luck, I decided to stop attempting to force the issue. I was guilty of trying too hard. Now, I'm just waiting for love to find me...or not.'

'How do you know that isn't what's happening right now?' I ask shrewdly. 'You know what they say. Life's what happens when you're busy making plans.'

Having run through their final set, the boys vacate the stage to enormous cheers, only to be dragged back into the spotlight for an encore by their wildly screaming home crowd. When the final chord has been played, the balcony empties and we return inside, ready to greet the band themselves, who are due to join us shortly. As always, the instant they enter the room there is uproar, as their greatest supporters fall upon them, showering each band member with congratulations.

'Come with me,' I mutter to Annabel. With a guiding hand beneath her elbow, I escort her into an adjoining, vacant room and close the door behind us. There will be plenty of time for her to meet them later, if that's what she wants, but right now, it is I who requires her full attention.

'Why have you brought me in here? The truth,' she adds meaningfully.

'Is the truth something you think you can handle?' I reply playfully.

'Trust me, I've experienced every form of rejection known to man. I can handle it.'

I glance at her quizzically, exceptionally confused. I feel this incredible strength of attraction towards her, yet she thinks I'm about to reject her? She must have had some truly crappy experiences in the past, for that to be her overwhelming conclusion. I'm not sure I could desire her more if I tried.

'Well, only if you're sure,' I reply. Moving closer, I press her up against the wall, gratified to hear the sound of a low, fraught whimper.

'The truth is, I've been fantasising about exploring every inch of your gorgeous body, since I caught an all too brief glimpse of it on the beach.'

'You weren't in your right mind then,' she stammers, flushing puce.

'No,' I agree. 'I clearly wasn't. Because I should have made my move then and there.'

'Your move?' she repeats in astonishment.

'Mmmmm.'

'And what move would that be?' she asks, although her expression suggests she's not sure she wants to know the answer.

'Do you want me to tell you or show you?' I growl, moving in even closer. I can practically feel her heart hammering in her chest. She looks like she's about to pass out.

'Um...'

She gazes up in disbelief, waiting for me to fill the silence for her, but I'm not letting her off the hook that easily. Instead, I simply smile back.

'Well?' I prompt at last. 'The truth...'

'Show me,' she eventually manages to croak. Her throat is undoubtedly parched, thanks to the swift, shallow gasps she's been inhaling.

'That will be my absolute pleasure. But first, kiss me,' I demand, so close that I'm breathing into her mouth. 'I'm not coming any closer than this. You're gonna have to be brave and make the final move.'

I'm so close that I can't focus properly on her facial features, but I'm aware of her eyes crinkling slightly, her breath fast and shallow. I realise that she hasn't verbally refused me this time, at least not yet. It feels like I'm making progress with this glorious woman who fascinates me so completely. Just then, I feel her soft hand move up and cup my stubbly jaw. A thrill flashes through me and causes me to grunt quietly in response; I certainly hadn't been expecting that. With incredible sensitivity and care, her soft mouth takes ownership of my plump top lip, pulling it inside, making me groan with need. Each time I feel her delicate tongue swipe over my skin, I'm aware of my erection throbbing urgently, growing harder and harder with every passing second.

Closing my eyes, I simply savour the sensations, as we both start to exhale increasingly strained breaths. And then I can hold back no longer. With a moan of despair, I trap her firmly against the wall with my powerful frame, swamping her with my pure physicality. Running my hands through her hair, my fingers link around to support the back of her head, as our tongues entwine and we pull each other ever closer. As though a fuse has been lit, our passion ignites, burning out of control as we grab and claw at each other. Each of us urgently requires more, yet in this room, we both appreciate that can't happen.

I don't know how long we remain there like that; I don't care. When we finally pull apart, both flushed and panting heavily, my cock is throbbing unbearably. I couldn't be harder if I tried. Leaning against the wall, I am extremely grateful for its solid, unerring bulk; my head feels woozy and light. This woman has as good as blown my mind. Backing away slightly, I stare down at her. No humour or smiles are exchanged between us any longer. Just raw, urgent need. I have no recollection of the kiss of life Annabel gave me yesterday, but I can't deny that she has just breathed life into me, in a way that no woman has ever done before.

'Can we go somewhere more private?' I demand. I know she wants this just as much as I do. You don't kiss like we just did, without some serious chemistry going on.

'I'd like that,' she admits breathlessly. 'Actually, I'd love that,' she quickly corrects.

'Me too,' I confirm. 'Yours or mine?'

'I think I'd prefer mine,' she says quietly.

'Let's go then,' I grin, taking her hand and leading her purposefully out of the hospitality area.

I admit to feeling slightly guilty about leaving the party when it's in full-flow, but not as guilty as I probably should. Besides, if things work out with Annabel like I hope they will, she can meet the guys any time and there will be a shed load more gigs for us to enjoy. But right now, it is I who requires her undivided attention. Just the thought of that practically takes my breath away. Right now, I can't think of a greater thrill than burying myself inside this amazing woman and providing her with more deliberately focussed pleasure than she has ever known. And that's what I intend to give her. I'm going to treat her so damn right, that she never hesitates to kiss me again.

CHAPTER 7

ANNABEL

I groan urgently, as Leo's hands encircle my back and make their teasing way down, to stroke across the top of my ass. Having made a swift escape from the concert, Leo drove like the wind back to mine. And now, here we are in my bedroom, enjoying the pleasures of which our mouths are capable, lying beside each other on my bed. I can't deny that Leo is the most incredible kisser; astonishingly, he makes me feel feminine, desirable, sexy, courageous and shameless, all at the same time.

It has been the story of my life. I seem biologically conditioned *not* to feel good about myself. Out of one hundred compliments I might receive, they are all instantly discarded upon the receipt of one negative comment. Never happy with my own appearance or abilities, unkind words hurt me deeply. Yet I don't allow that to show or to truly take hold. Instead, I maintain a complex relationship with food, where sweet treats offer me a transitory hit of comfort in an occasionally callous world. In an ironic twist, I know the sugar rush prevents me disappearing into an emotionally darker place, yet ultimately it does nothing for my figure, or my opinion of it. Incredibly though, none of my insecurities are afforded the slightest attention within Leo's embrace; I simply feel desired, wanted and for the first time in my life, attractive.

For the longest time, we ride a powerful wave of lust. His hands and mouth are playful and exploratory, yet never once pushing me outside of my comfort zone. Quite the opposite in fact; his apparent insistence to take it slowly is building up the most urgent desire inside me. I feel as horny as hell.

'Touch me,' I plead and even to my ears, I sound like a woman being dangled right on the very edge of what she can physically withstand.

'Mmmmm, not yet. The first time I touch you, I want you to be wetter than you've ever known.'

Just hearing Leo admit that causes my pussy to ache even more powerfully. Does he have any ideas what those wicked words, murmured intimately into my ear, do to my willpower?

'I'm already there!' I want to scream, but instead I bite back another guttural moan.

His hand slips behind my back and easily unclasps my bra. I'm so eager for him, I even assist with its removal, causing him to smile tenderly.

'God, you're perfect,' he sighs, generating a warmth inside my chest cavity that makes me glow with satisfaction. Reverently cupping my heavy breast, he guides an aching nipple towards his mouth. As his warm, wet skin meets mine, I swallow a gasp. It's a noise that quickly becomes a rumbling groan, when his warm, highly skilled tongue takes ownership of my sensitive hardened nub.

'Oh God!' I pant, as he exerts the most sublime pressure. Jets of pleasure shoot straight through me and all self-control threatens to vacate my trembling form.

Leo takes a long time to be satisfied with his work, at which point he moves across to my other breast, which is willing and waiting to accept this most delicious form of torture. By the time he's finished, I'm nothing but a panting, dripping mess beneath the sexiest guy I could ever imagine. For a moment, a fragment of doubt dares to enter my head, making me query Leo's real reason for being here. Why does he want *me*? But my uncertainty is quickly forgotten as he crawls back towards my mouth and overwhelms me with a kiss so demanding and passionate that I forget my own name, never mind any vague doubts I might have been experiencing.

His tongue slides slowly and confidently inside my mouth, and I reciprocate in kind. I can't help but imagine how such tender ministrations would feel upon another location of my body entirely. When he slightly repositions, I feel the solid, impressive length of him, digging against my thigh. Predictably, my pussy automatically clamps down hard, tighter and wetter than I have ever known, dying to experience his incredible touch first hand.

Breaking our kiss, Leo starts to progress his way back down. In a significant display of trust, when he unfastens my trousers and starts to ease them down, I don't fight him. On the contrary, with a moan which is accompanied by a roll of my hips, I actively encourage him. What has he done to me? This behaviour is so out of character, but he just makes me feel so passionately wanton. My panties swiftly follow suit and, before I know it, I am entirely naked before him, grinding against the bed in reaction to his palm which playfully circles my torso.

Gradually, his gently stroking hand progresses lower. As it runs over my thighs, my legs involuntarily spread in response. I feel my eyes close and roll back in my head, overwhelmed by the building sense of need. Right now, the only thing I desire, is to feel him sinking deep within me. I am incapable of thinking about anything else. I have been trapped by his potent spell, where he holds me, intoxicated and bewitched.

The first time his fingertips graze my wetness, I emit an animalistic cry. The intensity is simply too much. I'm trapped between urgently needing more, and yet never wanting this delicate, intimate, teasing caress to end. Slowly, he builds me up and I shudder and twitch in response. When one of his fingers glides easily inside me, I collapse against the pillow, believing I might pass out. In disbelief, I glance down at him, only to become trapped within his gaze. Without ever breaking our connection, Leo starts to nudge his thumb closer and closer to my throbbing, enlarged clit.

'Oh fuck!' I yelp, as the teasing becomes too much and he glides so close to where I need to feel him. Suddenly, he smiles at me. Altering the position of his hand, a second finger joins the first, forcing me to clamp down incredibly hard as my clit finally receives the attention it so richly deserves. My hips immediately shoot forwards in shock, frantic to absorb every ounce of gratification being so expertly bestowed upon me.

'Go on, baby,' growls Leo, undoubtedly seriously turned on. 'Come for me.'

'Oh! God! Please don't stop!' I implore, my head thrashing against the pillow, body squirming around Leo's incredibly talented fingers, aware that I'm starting to lose all sense of coordination. I can feel the taut tendons in my neck, my spine curving and straightening beneath the blissful sensations, every muscle tensed. I feel utterly out of control and frenziedly make a grab for anything within my reach, in the hope it might provide a solid base, amongst the sinking sands that surround me.

Clearly taking me at my word, Leo sets up an unfailing, mind-bending rhythm with his hand. With a smirk, he daringly drops his mouth, sucking my clit tenderly between his lips and delivering the most mind-blowing pleasure I have ever known. With a shriek of despair, an eruption of heat and feel-good hormones flood my writhing body. My release is violent, fraught and badly needed and Leo ensures that every last ounce of that orgasm is expertly milked. Collapsing back against the bed, I instantly feel relief flood me. That was, without doubt, the most sexually satisfying experience I've ever known, although to be fair, my past is scarcely littered with noteworthy conquests. Confusingly, Leo fingers are still moving and, ever so gradually, I can feel my body responding, as though hungry for more.

'What are you doing?' I manage to utter, surprised that my voice still works.

'You begged me not to stop,' he smiled. 'I'm just following your instructions.'

'I didn't mean...ever...' I gasp, before sensation overloads my brain and my ability to speak is removed.

'Then I suggest you're a little more specific in the future,' smirks Leo, clearly intent on driving me effortlessly towards another climax.

For the longest time, I am held in a mind-numbing harmony of blissful denial and pleasurable relief. At last, Leo liberates me from his control and wriggles his way northwards once more.

'Fuck, I can't wait to be inside you, my angel,' he groans, running his lips along my cheek, before encompassing my mouth with a light, teasing kiss. I can smell my arousal on his breath. I can taste it on his skin.

'Angel?' I whisper as we break apart, a chill creeping up my spine to tingle uncomfortably at the base of my skull.

'My guardian angel,' he clarifies, looking down at me tenderly.

I consciously attempt to push away my insecurities and destructive thoughts, but this time they persist in haunting me. Something has really bothered me about the way Leo referred to me as his guardian angel and I can feel the slow drip, drip, drip of uncertainty, as the thought starts to attack my positive vibes and upbeat mood. Eventually, I push him gently away, no longer enjoying the pleasurable activity I was previously savouring. My demons have taken charge once again.

CHAPTER 8

LEO

'What's wrong?' I ask gently. Clearly something is.

'I'm sorry,' she mutters, pulling the bedcovers over herself and rubbing a weary hand across her face. Naturally, I ease back a little, to provide some much-needed space.

'Do you wanna talk about it?' My personal preference is to let our bodies do the talking and, in my opinion, they were doing a damn good job of it. However, from her behaviour, it is clear that Annabel no longer agrees. I desperately try to recall what I might have said or done in the past few minutes, to cause this extreme reaction. I can only remember making her orgasm countless times and calling her an angel.

'Why are you here?' she asks me in a pained voice. 'Why do you want me? I'm not much to look at.'

Immediately, I feel my hackles rise. Partly from the callous way Annabel refers to herself, but also because of her assumption that the only attribute I might be interested in, is a perfect body or a pretty face.

'You're beautiful,' I state categorically, only to hear her grunt disbelievingly in response. 'I appreciate that some men might lie, in order to get what they want from a woman,' I continue, trying to keep my voice calm. 'But I'm not one of them. However, the thing that gives us away every time is the reaction of our bodies. They never lie.' I glance down towards my cock which, although still imprisoned within denim jeans is evidently standing to attention, throbbing painfully. Frankly, it would be torturous not to continue tonight. I am aching to make love to Annabel, but I attempt to keep my despair hidden. 'A lack of confidence in yourself isn't good, Sweetheart.'

'No, I agree, it isn't,' she replies, wriggling further away from me. 'But that's not what this is. I'm just applying my own life experience and injecting a little healthy reality into the equation.'

'Yeah?' Now I'm seriously confused.

'You should probably go,' she mutters, sounding like she's about to cry.

'I can go, if that's what you really want,' I agree, despite being surprised by her reaction. Not that it matters, I guess, but I can't remember being turned down by a girl in my entire adult life. Still, I want to wrap my arms around her and tell her everything is going to be okay, but I have a feeling that won't be well received at this precise juncture.

'I think it's best,' she confirms, wiping a lone tear angrily from her cheek. 'You may think you're being kind...you may think I'm what you want...'

'You are,' I interrupt, unable to hold myself back. 'And I can assure you, I wouldn't make out with someone due to *kindness*!'

'But...' she continues, as though my outburst hadn't taken place. 'Anything that happens here tonight will ultimately cause me more pain than pleasure. At least in the long run. I can't believe this is real. You won't feel the same way about me in a month's time.'

'You think I'm being fake?' I exclaim, still trying to keep my temper, despite a wave of frustrated confusion. 'This is crazy! You're not even going to give me a chance to show how much I desire you?'

'I don't think you're fake. I just think you feel a subliminal guilt towards me, for saving your life.'

'You're impossible!' I grin, shaking my head at her. At last I understand where all this is coming from and I feel relief. If I understand the problem, at least I stand a chance of being able to resolve it. 'How can I possibly argue against that?'

'Sorry,' she says with a shrug, looking so sad that I can scarcely bear it.

'Fine. I've got it!' I exclaim, suddenly grabbed by inspiration. 'I'm gonna prove you wrong.'

'How?'

'You'll see,' I beam, straightening my clothes and preparing to leave. 'But first, you're gonna give me a huge hug, and I'm going to promise you that everything will work out just fine.'

PERHAPS IT WAS A SOMEWHAT unorthodox plan but, in my defence, I believe it's already proving successful. I was never going to be able to strongarm Annabel into my way of thinking, or talk her round; she's far too wilful to allow that to happen. If she believes that within a month I'll lose interest in her, then it's down to me to prove she's wrong. To that end, I've done everything an attentive boyfriend might wish to, with the exception of experiencing physical contact. We share texts throughout every day, I've met her for incredibly innocent walks along the beach, or drinks in local cafes, and I might have sent one or two gifts in her direction too. What I haven't done, however, is so much as kiss her on the cheek.

And I'm delighted to report that in the past few days, cracks have certainly begun to starting to show in Annabel's resolve. Teasing her with my nearness, yet failing to succumb to our mutually felt desires, I can sense her frustration when we're together. It's almost killing me too, as each time I go to reach out for her, I am forced to suppress my own needs. But I've always been insanely strong willed and I know this is what needs to happen, in order to shatter the crazy belief she's operating under. As her obvious desire grows in strength, I struggle to mask the huge sense of contentment I feel as my plan plays out in the way I'd hoped. On the eighteenth day, I receive the text I'd been waiting for.

"Okay. You win. I need to see you."

I gaze down at the screen with a grin. I'm in the recording studio with the band today, although fortunately we're in the middle of a lunch break.

"See me? You see me all the time."

I chuckle as I press send. I can just imagine Annabel's frustrated expression when she reads my message. I know exactly what she means, and she knows that.

"Fine. I need to be with you."

Ah now, this is more like it.

"Your timeline was a month. We've haven't even hit three weeks yet."

Almost immediately, my phone rings and I pick up with a sense of satisfaction.

'What?' she demands, before I've even managed to say one word. 'You're determined to carry this on, even though I'm admitting defeat?'

'Absolutely,' I laugh, already starting to feel myself harden, simply upon hearing her voice. 'Hello, by the way.' But Annabel is clearly not willing to be distracted.

'You made me feel incredible the other week,' she admits breathily, referring to the precious fragment of time we'd spent making out on her bed.

'I'd barely got started,' I smile, dropping my voice slightly to ensure I'm not overheard. 'I promise I have the capability and the inclination to provide you with far more pleasure than that.'

'I feel so sexy right now, just thinking about the evening we spent together,' she groans, sounding like a woman on the very edge.

'Good. And I will keep making you feel sexy, because that's what you are.'

'But I feel...horny,' she clarifies shyly.

'What are you saying? You just want to use me for sex? To scratch an itch? Is that all I am to you?' I query innocently, trying to keep the amusement from my tone.

'No, of course not,' she huffs. She's not lying; she really is feeling horny. That knowledge pleases me, more than I'd like to admit.

'I'd be delighted to take you out to dinner tonight,' I reply. 'Pick you up at seven?'

'Thank you,' she sighs, sounding more relieved than she has any right to be.

'But no funny business. You've still got twelve days to wait, until I officially lose interest in you.' Smiling, I hang up, just able to hear Annabel's disbelieving protests down the line. And now, thanks to the conversation matter, I'm as hard as iron.

CHAPTER 9

ANNABEL

This is unbearable. We've been seeing each other fairly continuously since the first day we met and even a blind man would be able to sense the uninhibited attraction that zings between us with every glance. And yet Leo seems determined to prove his point and make me wait, even though waiting is the very last thing I want to be doing. We've just finished our meal when he takes my hand, and lifts it to his mouth. In full view of the restaurant, he drops an open-mouthed kiss on my palm, before dragging his teeth across my sensitive skin, just to increase the level of torment. Closing my eyes, I funnel all of my concentration into not crying out, aware that arousal has started to pool in my panties.

'I know what you're doing,' I grunt, as he finally releases me from his spell. He's teasing me with his nearness, flirting with all my senses. But apparently it isn't enough for him, that I concede and admit I was wrong about him, because I've already done that. He wants me to suffer the agony of appreciating that he really does desire me, without being permitted to do a thing about it. Grudgingly, I have to admit it is genius...in a fairly twisted kind of way.

'And is it working?' he murmurs, knowing full well it is.

'Put it like this,' I admit, in a flash of unusual frankness. 'Right now, I can't work out if I want to strangle you or fuck you.'

'Only twelve more days and we can find out,' he laughs.

'Seriously, can't we stop this now?'

'Seriously, no we can't. You doubted the strength of my attraction to you. There are a lot of things I'll take lying down, but that's not one of them.'

'You can't blame me,' I argue, ignoring his hefty double entendre. 'You could have any woman you wanted.'

'I'm pretty sure that's not true, but even if it is, I'm looking at my choice right now.'

I send Leo a sideways glance that suggests I don't believe him entirely, but will accept what he's saying for the sake of a peaceful evening. After all, tonight isn't the first time we've shared this conversation.

'You need me to remind you why again?' he asks shrewdly.

'No!' I complain, as he starts to list the huge number of positive attributes which I apparently exhibit, ticking each one off his fingers in turn. I'm sure half of them don't apply to me and I can feel my cheeks flushing deeper and deeper, in response to his complimentary words.

'And then, of course, the most important reason of all,' he adds for good measure, at the end.

'What's that?' I ask meekly, pretty sure I don't want to know.

'That I choose you out of guilt, because you saved my life.'

'Oh piss off,' I groan in mock frustration, as he laughs heartily, clearly pleased with himself.

'Too soon?'

'*Way* too soon,' I smile, shaking my head at his antics.

'I'm glad you're starting to appreciate how truly ridiculous that sounds. Shall we make a move?'

Rising to his feet, Leo briefly adjusts his clothing, pulling his shirt down slightly. With a secret smile, I think I know why. He wants to hide the bulge of his erection from public view. I can't help but sense a spark of hope flickering inside me; if he wants me as much as I want him tonight, surely I can persuade him to break his rule?

'Your house is just down the road,' I observe innocently, as my hand slips into his and we stroll out of the restaurant together.

'So it is. Want a coffee. Or something?' he asks meaningfully.

'Yeah. Or something,' I confirm, biting my lower lip in delicious expectation of exactly what he might mean.

HIS DESIRES BECOME IMMEDIATELY APPARENT, the second the door of his home closes behind us. Fortunately, by lucky chance, they mirror my wishes entirely.

'I need you,' I groan wantonly, as he steps closer, his hand stroking the curve of my waist. My hands automatically reach for his taut, muscled body and I pull him closer still.

'I know exactly what you need,' he grunts. 'Don't worry about that. Only twelve days to wait until you get it.'

'Please,' I beg, aware that I'm breathing heavily, as passion overwhelms any reservations or self-control I might have been hanging on to. 'I need to fuck you. Now.'

'Do you?' His words are said in such a low, self-confident growl that I fear my legs might buckle beneath me. Fortunately at that moment, Leo pushes me back against the wall, trapping me with his powerful torso and pinning me upright.

I start to pant as he cups my jaw, a smile daring to flirt around his lips. Temptingly, he runs a thumb down my exposed throat, causing me to swallow hard in anticipation.

'I wanted you eighteen days ago and I was denied,' he whispers against my ear, causing a shudder of lust to blast down my neck and shoulders. I hear myself whimper uncontrollably, as his hands search out the curve of my ass and squeeze gently. 'Perhaps I should deny you now?'

'No!' I groan. No longer able to cope with the havoc this man is wreaking, I slump back against the wall and allow my eyes to close, as my head rolls back in surrender. But Leo isn't done torturing me yet.

'Get you to the point of no return and then send you home, like you did to me?'

'Please – no.'

'If you want my mercy tonight, I'll need you to promise one thing.'

'Anything!' I gasp, meaning it. I am desperate to make love to this man.

'You never question my motives for wanting to be with you again. And you don't say you're somehow less worthy than any other person. You don't even think it.'

Swallowing hard, I nod.

'I promise,' I say somberly.

'Then kiss me,' he demands, in a tone that fills my entire being with lust. Instantly, my eyes are open and fully focussed. 'And do it like you mean it.'

'Deal,' I purr, my face breaking out into a huge smile as my hand slides into his.

'Deal,' he confirms, displaying a marked softening of his tone.

'But first, follow me.'

Ignoring Leo's confused look, I guide him through his house, up the stairs and into a large, airy bedroom. Encouraging him to sit on the king-sized bed, I take a step backwards and slowly begin to unbutton my blouse. The expression on his face, delightedly drinking me in, gives me all the encouragement I require to continue. When I'm down to just my black lace underwear, I make my way daringly closer. Thanks to a gentle push I give his chest, Leo lies down. Quickly, I straddle his hips, able to feel his swollen length pressing against my delicate, increasingly sensitive flesh. A small moan escaping from Leo's throat sends a shot of courage through me. His hands tenderly caress my thighs and I lean forwards and follow his clear instruction.

The instant our lips meet, I am hit by a confusing array of emotions; happiness, ecstasy, intense arousal and just the overwhelming sense of rightness; we are meant to be. Our kiss very quickly descends into something incredibly raw and dirty, as our tongues tease each other's mouths suggestively, hands exploring everywhere they can reach. Before I know it, although our mouths haven't yet separated, all of our clothes are littering the bedroom floor. Leo is on top, his weight pressing me down into the mattress, making me feel trapped in a position that I have absolutely no wish to be released from.

'Fuck,' he pants, breaking our kiss to slide down to my chest. 'Do you have any idea how much I need you?'

'Oh! God!' I cry, as the sensation of his mouth taking a firm grasp around my hard, aching nipple threatens to overwhelm me. The feeling is entirely mutual; I have never desired another human being as much as I want Leo right now. My fingers slide through his hair, cradling the back of his skull and encouraging him on. At the same time, I manage to open my legs slightly and wrap them around his incredible body. His mouth is incredibly skilled, making full use of his tongue, teeth and lips to heighten my arousal, sending jets of pleasure shooting straight to my abdomen, creating a warm, wet heat.

'I need to taste you,' he groans urgently, shuffling further down.

'No!' I cry, wriggling out from beneath him. 'You first.' He instructed me to kiss him like I meant it, and I'm not through with the challenge he set me yet. Not by a long shot. I push him back onto the bed, unprepared for the sight before me. For the first time, I am seeing Leo naked...and the vision is a glorious one. My eyes are inevitably drawn towards his cock; straining, throbbing, twitching. There is no doubt in my mind what he needs.

With a secret smile, I wiggle down the bed until my head is adjacent to his groin. I hear him inhale swiftly as my soft hand takes hold of his impressive length. Glancing up at his face, I am met by a focussed yet tender gaze. Subconsciously, I lick my lips, already able to feel the saliva gathering in my mouth, thanks to the sheer, desperate need I have to taste him. Lowering my head, my eyes naturally close and a low groan of pleasure escapes my throat.

CHAPTER 10

※

LEO

'Ann...uh...' I grunt, my eyes wide open in disbelief that this is about to happen. I want to make some virtuous and noble statement that she isn't obliged to do this, despite my earlier demand that she kisses me like she means it. This truly wasn't what I had in mind. However, both the words and the sentiment remain unspoken, as speech fails me. Besides, from the look on her face, I reckon she's already seriously enjoying herself. This is not an act of duty. Annabel is already more than I ever imagined she would be.

In slow motion, I watch incredulously as her mouth opens slightly, hovering just above my painfully aching cock. I can feel every breath from her lungs, as it bounces across my pulsating head and races down the shaft. I was already as hard as hell, thanks to the fraught pressure that's been building up between us all evening, but this is making things ten times more agonising. My desperation has inundated every single thought in my mind; I'm seriously struggling to contemplate anything else but this woman, in this moment. It makes me smile that Annabel thinks I was seriously capable of sticking to our thirty day agreement and turn her down tonight. She doesn't know me that well yet, but she will soon.

The first touch of her mouth is pure heaven. With a groan, I close my eyes as my hips naturally set up a slow, continuous rocking. My ass presses into the mattress with every movement I make, assisting with the rhythm, helping to edge me further and further inside. As her mouth and hands get to work, it almost becomes too much. I can feel the uncontained heat in my groin, able to sense pre-cum starting to leak into her willing mouth.

Far too quickly, she leads me readily to the boundary of my self-control. Unwillingly, my hands reach down to stop her as I wriggle backwards.

'Anna...' I gasp, her face swimming unfocussed before me, as I urgently try to regain my senses. 'This first time...I desperately want to come inside you.'

'Mmmmm,' she sighs, using her finger to lightly remove my arousal from her lips, before sucking it into her mouth. The sight is too much for me. With a groan like a wild animal, I pull her mouth to mine and devour her right there on the spot. My kiss is demanding, forceful and urgent and she responds in kind. But I need more. I must have more.

Ripping my mouth from hers, I nip down her luscious body, revelling in the shrieks of passion I inspire, as I head towards her pussy. I can already smell her, but I need to taste.

'Your turn,' I mutter.

'Oh fuck!' she yelps, as I plant my teeth high up on her inner thigh, already slippery with her wetness. 'Jeez-us!' she screams, as I switch across to the other, before sliding my tongue straight through her warm, wet folds, from ass to clit. She tastes tangy yet sweet and I know that it will be impossible to ever get enough of her.

Just from reading her responses, I'm fully aware that neither of us are in any mood for slow and teasing. Like the lid clattering noisily on a boiling saucepan, our desire has reached the uncontainable stage and it is imperative we act. Yet still, I desire her pleasure even more than my own. With that in mind, I wrap my lips around her swollen clit and suck gently as my fingers set to work.

Gasping, Annabel gyrates continuously against my mouth. It takes an impressively short time for her to disintegrate into the first of many orgasms that night. I'm almost overwhelmed with the sheer power and intensity of pleasure that the act yields and immediately, I am driven to experience it again. And again. And again.

'Need... to... rest...' she gasps eventually, causing me to smile. Watching her chest expand and contract powerfully, I accept that I might be guilty of getting a little carried away.

'Poor baby,' I murmur, wriggling up her body. Gently, I ease my thickened cock to slide through her swollen lips and hold still. 'Talk to me about contraception.'

'I'm on the pill,' she gasps, rolling her hips to try and gain more of what she requires. Inevitably, the sensations of me holding myself so near, but yet so far, quickly become too much.

'You went on it for me, didn't you?' I ask shrewdly, feeling very honoured that she trusted me enough to purposefully take this action. From previous conversations, I know she hasn't had an active sex life in recent years.

'Yeah,' she grunts, unafraid to look me directly in the eye.

'Mmmmm, good girl,' I sigh. 'Let me reward you.' Slowly inching myself deeper, I know from her desperate moans of delight that I'm stretching her, pushing her to the furthest limits.

Purposefully, my entry is extremely slow. I neither want to alarm or hurt her. The instant our groins mesh and I know I've reached the very deepest extent possible, we both groan with incredible satisfaction. We fit together perfectly, just like I knew we would. Sliding back, I commence with a slow, steady set of thrusts that feel like nothing I've ever known before. From the way Annabel is writhing beneath me, I have an inkling that she's of a similar mind. Despite only being a mere mortal, right now I'm in heaven and simply never want this to end.

Regardless of my good intentions, the situation escalates fast and we deteriorate into rampant fucking. Nothing is off limits; no request denied, every position explored. There is no doubt that the past eighteen days have taken their toll on both of us and we are now revelling in the freedom to experience what we have been actively craving. I know that later tonight, we will enjoy each other slowly and tenderly.

At that point, we will truly make love. But for now, this is exactly what we desire, and we both accept that.

With my hand wound through Annabel's long hair, I hold her firmly in position. On her elbows and knees, I know she feels very vulnerable and exposed to my deep, pounding thrusts from behind. She's been orgasming fairly continuously for some time now and I've started to move beyond the point of no return. The ache in my cock has reached unbearable levels and a tingling has commenced in my balls, which continue to rhythmically slap against her soaked skin.

'I'm gonna come,' I grunt in despair, raising my voice slightly to be heard above her very vocal sounds of pleasure.

And then suddenly, as though my statement has unchained me, my hips thrust unreservedly into Annabel's open, pliant body. I am finally free to let go. Releasing her hair, I firmly grab onto her soft, rounded hips, my fingers digging demandingly into her flesh. With a low, long moan, I power myself forwards, pulling her back hard to meet me; an action which automatically results in another climax from the incredible woman I am sharing this with. Experiencing an overwhelming sense of relief, I finally surrender. Having pumped every single drop of my seed into Annabel's convulsing, twitching body, we both collapse onto the bed. Pulling her into my embrace, there I remain, cuddling her from behind, savouring the continued joy of being inside her. So wet, so tight, so mine.

EPILOGUE

ANNABEL

Leo and I have been dating for about six months now and we are definitely still in the honeymoon period. I swear I've never felt so happy, complete or exhausted! Although we continue to maintain two separate homes, I'm honestly not sure how long that will last; we seem to spend every spare hour with each other. Despite that, I still can't get enough of him.

Right now I'm in my car, on my way to Babe Beach to meet him. Unusually, we're travelling separately because he's been working hard in the recording studio all morning, followed by a radio interview this afternoon. He's making quite a name for himself as a songwriter, as interest in his work continues to grow all the time, and I couldn't be more proud. His latest song was written from the depths of his soul. Coupled with a killer melody, it is a genuine, heartfelt love story which has captured the imagination of fans across the world.

Just then, a song I know well comes onto the radio and I find myself reaching for the volume button, in order to crank it right up. It's the current number one charting song in the UK, America and fifteen other countries across the world. Each and every time I hear it, I can sense tears forming as my throat constricts. Entitled *You Saved Me*, quite simply, the song is breathtaking in its beauty.

As I reach my destination, I observe my tall, blond, handsome boyfriend leaning casually against his car. The moment he sees me approaching, his face lights up in recognition, and I can't help but beam back. Having parked up, I glance over to see Leo striding confidently in my direction. The look he gives me sends shivers through my entire body. There is no doubt in my mind what he wants, but he'll have to wait. We're going swimming first...at Babe Beach, no less. Not that we always swim here, but it has at least become an alternative location to visit. For at long last, I appreciate that beauty is a lot more than whether you've got a fat ass or not. Leo's been a major influence in altering my mindset; he loves me for who I am, and has helped me to have pride in my appearance. Besides, when the sexiest guy on the beach is showering you with love and affection, it becomes surprisingly easy to accept that you must have at least a few positive attributes.

I switch off the engine and allow the final chorus of the tune to come to an end. By this time, Leo has reached me. Squatting down beside my car door, he leans in against the open window. The lyrics float across the perfect scene, breathing life into everything. *Enduring love through stormy seas, you saved me.* Every time I hear the song play, my mind skips back to the scribbled words Leo wrote on my notepad, at the gig we'd attended all those months earlier.

'Great choice of song,' he grins, the soft hair lying across his forehead being lifted slightly by the gentle sea breeze.

'Thanks,' I agree contentedly, happiness literally oozing from my pores, knowing the man I love did eventually manage to find his inspiration. 'This seriously hot guy wrote it for me.'

THE END

BLAST FROM THE PAST

FENELLA ASHWORTH

CHAPTER 1

JANE

Toby Jacobs had always been hot. Like, *seriously* hot. Even when we were kids, and I really shouldn't have been lusting over my brother's best friend, it was an unassailable truth. Not that anything ever happened between us; he was way too busy snogging his way through the rest of the school. Besides, I don't believe he ever saw me as anything other than Mike's annoying little sister. And that was fine by me, obviously. I didn't seek his attention anyway...well, not very much. But it came as absolutely no surprise to discover that a television channel had snapped him up as the celebrity component of the next *Celebrity Blast from the Past* show.

Merging carefully onto the fast motorway, my mind momentarily focuses entirely on the road ahead. However, it doesn't take long for the monotony of driving at seventy miles per hour along a relatively straight road, to take effect, allowing Toby to float back into my thoughts. In all honesty, I haven't set eyes on him for...I don't know how long. It didn't help that when he went away to university, he never returned to live in our hometown. Although I have briefly chatted to him at a few parties over the years; he's a close family friend, after all. And of course, Toby is still regularly in touch with my brother, so occasional snippets of gossip have been forthcoming from that source, over the passing of the years.

A huge sign flashes past, informing me that Central London is now just eighteen miles away and not for the first time, I wonder whether I'm making an enormous mistake. Taking a deep breath, I push my foot a little more firmly down on the throttle; goodness only knows why I agreed, but I've committed to attending and I never back out on my word. But the truth of the matter is, I'm somewhat terrified. You see, Toby isn't the only one who was approached to star on *Celebrity Blast from the Past*. They want me there too. Let me explain.

The premise of what is a truly weird, but still very popular show is quite straightforward. A celebrity is joined on stage by three anonymous people, each seated behind a screen. They can only be viewed in silhouette and their identities are entirely obscured. The three screens are labelled Past, Present and Future. The person behind the 'Past' screen is someone the celebrity knew a long time ago; the role I will be fulfilling today. The person behind the 'Present' screen is somebody the celebrity has known only in recent years, while the 'Future' screen is someone they don't know at all. God only knows how they go about picking the future person; just stick a pin in a telephone directory and chance their luck, I guess. The celebrity then chooses one of the three to go on a blind date weekend with, accompanied by a camera crew, obviously...

I mean, it's utter bollocks. Plus, given we occasionally bump into each other, I'm not in Toby's past. Or at least, I hope I'm not because he's a good guy. No, wait. That's an understatement. He's a great guy in all honesty. Kind, decent and thanks to a killer set of dimples in his cheeks, in possession of a smile that could light up a room. It's probably why the ladies always fall for him and he's never been one to say no; women are definitely his weakness. I guess I should be grateful that nothing did ever happen between us. Much better for us to be on continued speaking terms, rather than registering as just another notch on his bedpost, which must be more sawdust than post by now.

I pull into the car park of the production company, doing my best to take deep steadying breaths. Unfortunately, I'm not sure they're achieving anything, other than making me feel increasingly light-headed. Almost immediately, I find myself whisked up a darkened corridor and into my own dressing room. This programme is made by a huge broadcasting conglomerate, capable of maintaining a level of secrecy of which the British government would be rightly proud. Mind you, that probably isn't saying much. These days, the government apparently has more leaks than a cheap toilet.

'Miss Green?' says a voice, accompanied by a brisk knock.

'Hello,' I reply, spinning around to face the door. A somewhat harassed looking woman enters, carrying a clipboard and a walkie talkie.

'Hi! I'm Sandra. I'm here to look after you today. This is Alice. She'll be doing your hair and makeup,' she adds, as an immaculate young woman breezes into the room and takes up position beside the mirror.

'Ah, I don't normally wear makeup,' I explain. I'm afraid I've always been a *what you see is what you get* kind of person, and that includes forcing people to observe my haggard, thirty-four year old face as nature intended. Ironically, my attitude probably stems from being called 'Plain Jane' by Mike and Toby as a kid; I accepted their teasing as a badge of honour and defiantly carried my outlook through to adulthood.

'It's required for the cameras,' explains Sandra patiently.

'But why bother? I'll be behind a screen, won't I?' For once in my life, I'm not trying to be purposefully difficult. It's a valid question.

'Only if he doesn't choose you,' she beams, sending me a playful wink.

In utter shock, I allow myself to be led towards the dressing table, where Alice leaps into action. It probably sounds stupid, but I honestly hadn't considered that Toby might actually select me as his blind date. I mean, we've gone through our entire lives together without him showing any interest, so it hadn't dawned on me that behind a screen and with my voice slightly distorted, I might actually end up being his type. Unexpectedly, a powerful bubble of excitement traverses my body, exploding uncomfortably at the back of my neck, where it sets each and every hair standing to attention.

Before I know it, in my dazed confusion, I am led down countless corridors before finally being admitted into the back of a warm, airy studio. Directed straight into one of the booths, I don't catch sight of the audience, although the excited buzz inevitably produced by a large number of people is unmistakable. Thoughtfully, a small screen has been installed in the booth, allowing me to observe the show, so I do my best to settle back and relax.

'Microphone test,' says a voice, which is unexpectedly pumped through the speakers into my booth, making me visibly jump.

'Miss Past?'

'Y...yes,' I stutter, my pulse ramping up several gears as my input is required. I'm such a knob. This is such a bad idea.

'Just a practice question to test the microphone,' explains the voice soothingly. 'What are your hobbies?'

'Er...work, family,' I reply, suddenly realising how incredibly mundane I sound. I'd be so much more fascinating if I illegally base jumped off tall buildings or was training to swim across the English Channel to France. 'And I try to keep fit.'

'And do you regularly run?' they continue, the sound levels clearly not yet to their satisfaction.

'Yeah,' I sigh, rubbing my forehead in frustration. 'Out of patience, fucks and money.'

Immediately, I hear the crowd howl in amusement, accompanied by several isolated claps. I realise, to my horror, that my retort has just been broadcast to everyone.

'The microphone's working fine,' confirmed the producer, sounding slightly disgruntled. 'But Miss Past, we can't transmit responses like that, so please contain your language, once recording starts?'

'Of course...sorry.'

As with all things, dreading an event only makes it occur even sooner than anticipated. Before I know what's happening, the lights are adjusted, the title music is blaring through the speakers and I'm feeling more than a little nauseous. The obedient audience burst into noisy applause and Cherry, a well-known female presenter, explodes onto the stage wearing the most alarming coloured jacket in the history of mankind.

'Goooooooood Evening!' Cherry exclaims in a grinding voice that is guaranteed to get on my nerves within seconds, rather than minutes. 'And welcome to Ceeeeeee-lebrity Blast from the Past!' Where the fuck did they find this woman? She is beyond annoying. Having made a big spectacle of introducing Toby, I can't help but lean forward and observe the screen closely. He walks confidently onto the stage and takes a seat beside her as the crowd goes wild. Yep. He's still as hot as ever. At least Cherry seems to think so; she is barely attempting to contain her adulation. Tall, dark-haired, a physique to die for and the most incredible blue eyes you could literally lose yourself in, I can just imagine women fawning over him, wherever he goes. Except for me, of course. Any admiration I might, or might not have for the man, has always been kept fully under wraps.

'Time for your first question,' murmurs Cherry, smiling hungrily up at him. Toby gets to ask three questions of us, after which he is required to make his choice.

'Ah, my first question is very easy, actually,' he replies, the deep timbre in his voice sending a powerful surge through my abdomen that I seriously wasn't prepared for. 'I would like to experience one kiss with each lady.'

I gasp as an ice-cold sensation fills my brain. They surely aren't going to permit this?

'Well, that certainly is most unorthodox!' splutters Cherry, visibly knocked out of her habitual cool. 'Why?'

'Because a kiss is more revealing than a thousand words, don't you think?' he murmurs, and I visibly observe her falling under his spell.

Unbelievably, after a brief pause where our permission is obtained to take part in this somewhat unusual request, I watch in disbelief as a blindfolded Toby is led into my booth and we are left alone. Well, apart from the multitude of people and cameras observing our silhouettes from the studio, that is. We have strict instructions not to exchange any words, but that honestly isn't a problem. I'm not capable of speaking right now, even if I wanted to.

The first thing I'm truly aware of is his physicality; he towers over me and it feels as though I'm being asked to share my previously safe space with an Apex predator. I feel vulnerable, in danger...hunted. The next thing my overstimulated body picks up on is his scent. God, this close up, he smells divine. I start to salivate, experiencing an overwhelming urge to taste his skin for myself, just to be sure. Blindly reaching out for my face, he manages to cradle my trembling jaw tenderly, before leaning towards me in a practiced way. His skin feels warm and soft, sending a powerful surge of arousal straight through the centre of my core, making the backs of my thighs feel inexplicably weak. As his lips hover millimetres above my own, I'm aware that we are sharing the same air and I involuntarily emit a long, low groan of desire. And then our mouths join, and I am lost.

CHAPTER 2

TOBY

Seriously what on God's green earth was I thinking when I signed up for this farce? I find myself wincing slightly when Cherry announces a commercial break; the woman is an utter moron. She'd be well advised to stop fluttering her eyelids at me and try keeping her hands to herself too. If she attempts to squeeze my thigh one more time, I swear I'll scream. Perhaps the most annoying aspect to the entire programme is that I'm being billed as a 'celebrity', when nothing could be further from the truth.

Referring to me as a celebrity is a major overstatement. I'm just a normal bloke who was in the right place at the right time. The previous winter, I witnessed a young girl fall into a flooded river near where I live. I was fortunate to be close enough to dive in and grab hold of her. Despite the powerful current, I managed to keep us both afloat until the rescue helicopter arrived. Thankfully, both Christie and I were then winched to safety. Against my wishes, the incident made the local papers and later the national news. I'm certainly not one to court publicity, but I fear the press have been somewhat infatuated with me ever since.

When the television producers first approached me to take part in this show, I turned them down outright. They returned, offering a donation to the Search and Rescue team that saved us. The amount being bandied around was capable of keeping the charity running for the better part of six months. Even at the time, I fully appreciated their offer was a form of emotional blackmail. Yet, a serious amount of money was being offered, which I honestly didn't feel I had the right to refuse. Now, I'm wishing I'd found another way to raise those funds.

'Fantastic job,' purrs Cherry, attempting to caress my thigh yet again. This time, I'm alert to it, capturing her wrist and assertively returning it back to her side. She looks at me curiously before continuing. 'Once we start recording again, it will be time for you to select which lady you wish to go on a blind date with. Are you ready to do that?'

'I am,' I confirm, hoping she'll leave me alone to review my decision. I've asked all three questions now, but to be honest, kissing each of the women was the most telling part of our communication. After that, my other questions were practically rendered obsolete.

The first woman, who apparently represents my past, is causing me the greatest concern. Our kiss was actually pretty amazing; passionate, honest and seriously arousing. I can only assume that she's an ex from my school days, who's got a damn sight better at kissing since then. I'd definitely have remembered her otherwise. The truth is, I had many, *many* conquests as a young lad. What's the equivalent word for a slutty guy? A player? A womaniser? A man-whore? Well, whatever it is, that was me. I admit to being ashamed of my younger behaviour now, not that there's much I can do to change my past. Thank God, with age comes maturity and self-awareness. And part of my maturity ensures that I will never return to a previous relationship, which is the overriding reason I won't be selecting Miss Past. But she intrigues me; boy does she intrigue me.

Using exactly the same logic, I won't be selecting contestant number two either, who allegedly represents my present. Within seconds of kissing her, it became horribly clear that she was none other than Florence, a psycho ex-girlfriend. She's been trying to edge her way back into my life for months now, with a zero success rate.

The instant I realised what I was dealing with, I hastily made my exit from her booth; no way am I opening up that can of worms again.

Which by process of elimination leaves me with number three as my blind date; Miss Future. In all honesty, I'm probably allowing my cock to select this woman; our kiss was full of natural passion and depth of feeling. With zero reservations, she kissed me like her life depended on it. If I were to allow my head, or even my heart to select my blind date, I can't deny my thoughts keep returning to Miss Past in the first booth. But that is not to be. Before I know it, we're back on air and I'm being asked to confirm my choice.

'I'd like to go on a blind date with Miss Future, please.'

Instantaneously, the audience breaks out into raucous cheers, as though my decision matters on an emotional level to them. I honestly don't see how it can do, when it doesn't even resonate emotionally for me. As far as I'm concerned, this is all about the money.

'In that case, thank you very much Miss Past and Miss Present. If you could leave us now?'

'Hang on!' I mutter in an undertone, as they disappear unseen out the back of their booths. 'You mean, I don't get to find out who they were?'

'I'm afraid those are the rules,' beams Cherry smugly, possibly trying to repay me for my clear rejection of her advances earlier on. 'Because you've chosen Miss Future! Come and join us, Mary!' she exclaims, as the silhouette in the third booth stands up and makes her way towards us.

'Jesus Christ!' I exclaim loudly, within seconds of seeing her face. Before Mary's got anywhere near me, I turn on my heel and storm out of the studio in the opposite direction, leaving Cherry mouthing like an abandoned goldfish.

I march back to my dressing room in double-time and start to gather my belongings together. I feel furious...used even. However, my departure is delayed by most of the production crew piling into the room behind me.

'Is there a problem here?' enquires the producer, evidently attempting to appear calm but sounding anything but. I roll my eyes in a somewhat condescending manner. Seriously, this entire situation defies belief.

'If that woman turns out to be part of my future, then God help me!' I exclaim, pacing the room angrily.

'I'm sorry, Toby, but I'm failing to see the...'

'She's a Goddamn nutcase! I've got a restraining order in place against her!' I bellow, feeling surprisingly satisfied at the look of abject horror which passes over the expressions of the assembled gathering. 'I mean, for fuck's sake! Didn't anyone screen these women?'

It was about three months ago when Mary Saunders started appearing at random and unexpected times during the day. When I was out shopping, going to the gym or visiting my parents. Then she started loitering outside my home, hanging around my car. After failing to successfully plead with her verbally, enough eventually became enough and I was forced to get a restraining order. Which, incidentally, she is breaking at this very moment, simply from knowingly being in the same building as me. In my mind, Mary's presence is yet another negative side effect of the publicity I've been subjected to; doesn't anyone see the real me anymore?

'We'll reshoot the end segment,' offers the producer. 'Then you can choose an alternative woman.'

'And we'll double the money being donated to your charity,' added another company representative, as a sweetener. From his glasses, bald head and clipboard, I assume he's the finance guy. I'm not ignorant to the fact that the advertising revenues in the commercial breaks alone, when this episode screens, ensure they are willing to go all out. Come hell or high water, they need me to select a partner and go on a blind date.

'Well, I'm not exactly left with much choice, am I? Given that Miss Present in booth number two is my psycho ex!'

'Who the hell's responsible for research?' growled one of the suits. Clearly, heads were going to roll later today.

'How do you know it's her?' demanded Cherry, who had edged her way unseen into the room.

'Like I said, you can tell a lot from a kiss.'

'Miss Past, then?' suggested the producer, looking increasingly desperate. 'You don't know who *she* is, do you?'

I shake my head in response.

'Then we'll call her back!'

'One second,' I announce, raising a finger in the air before the entire crew disappears. 'How much is she getting paid to take part in this charade?'

Finance guy responds, mentioning a sum of money so paltry, that my jaw visibly drops in astonishment.

'You need to pay her ten grand,' I demand. And I don't feel guilty about requesting it either. They're a big company and can more than afford the outlay.

'That's not how this works...'

'Well, that's how it's gonna have to work this time.'

'She gets two nights away with you, all expenses covered, as her payment,' explains Cherry in a manner that makes me feel as though I must have a negative I.Q.

'I'm not sure many people would consider that adequate recompense,' I laugh coldly. Besides, I'm normally pretty easy going, and even I'd be pissed to discover I'm someone's third choice out of three for a date. If we've got to spend several days together, the financial inducement is as much for my benefit as hers. 'I've told you what my terms are. Either double the charity donation and pay up ten grand, or I walk.'

I receive a number of furtive glances. Some of them are admiring, others entirely unimpressed. With a heavy sigh, the producer grabs the walkie talkie from his belt.

'I need to speak with Miss Past,' he demands, sounding none too happy.

'She's already left the building,' a fuzzy, muffled voice responds.

'Then I suggest you track her down, pretty damn fast!'

CHAPTER 3

JANE

'Wait up!' calls a harassed-sounding woman. I briefly glance backwards to see her jogging in my direction, before returning all focus to my handbag. In my emotional state, I've tipped its contents all over the tarmac, yet I'm still completely unable to locate my car keys. I'm sure it meant fuck all to Toby, but I gave absolutely everything to our kiss. At the time, it had felt like I had nothing to lose, so I allowed all of the feelings I'd bottled up over the decades to be released in the most honest exchange of my life. And despite that, even with my appearance hidden and my voice distorted, he'd still chosen another woman over me. I guess my personality simply isn't what he desires. And as much as I'm angry with myself for feeling this way, his rejection still hurts like hell.

'I'm really sorry,' gasps the woman, hand on chest as her lungs recover from an unanticipated sprint. 'But we need you to come back inside.'

'Why?' I'm honestly not in the mood for this and the last thing I want now is to accidentally bump into Toby. As it stands, if I can escape unseen, he'll never know I took part in this programme. He'll never know we kissed. The secret will be mine, and mine alone. Then, I'll only have my own personal embarrassment to contend with. But the longer I hang around here, the higher the chance of discovery becomes. If only I hadn't misplaced my sodding keys, I'd already be on my way.

'Miss Future ended up having a restraining order in place against her. We have to reshoot the end.'

'Just get him to select the other one. You don't need me there for that.'

'There's kind of a problem with her too...she's his ex.'

'So I'm his last choice?' I confirm. As if I didn't already know that.

'Yes. We'll pay you. Ten thousand pounds,' the woman adds quickly. The initial look on my face must have made it crystal clear what my thoughts were about returning, but I can't help pausing to consider her offer. It's an enormous sum of money. I only wish I were in a position to refuse it.

'Has he worked out who I am?'

'No,' she confirms. 'It will be a shock when we re-record.' You're telling me, love. 'There aren't any skeletons in your closet too, are there?' she asks in a manner of someone not really wanting to know the answer. 'Our background checks have been about as useful as a chocolate teapot on this occasion.'

'No, don't worry,' I sigh. 'I'm probably one of the few people in the world he does actually trust...or did once, anyway.

'Aaaaaaannnnd, you've chosen Miss Past! Come and join us, Jane!' exclaims Cherry, delighting in announcing the big reveal. I have to give her some credit; she displays no indication of the mayhem that's taken place over the past hour.

Feeling a strange combination of sick, dizzy and utterly mortified, I rise from the stool, giving my legs a second to stop wobbling. Cautiously, I step out of the booth, instantly blinded by the studio lights, totally dreading the moment that Toby sees me. As I walk towards him and our eyes meet for the first time, I witness his initial expression of sheer delight upon realising it is me. His smile swiftly fills me with confident optimism, as my stomach unexpectedly dissolves with lust.

But that euphoric state doesn't last very long. Within seconds, he is looking at me with something akin to horrified astonishment, as reality asserts itself. Yes. We did. We shared *that* kiss. His expression is excruciating to witness. Immediately, I feel the floor fall away from me, taking all my self-worth, courage and confidence with it. Still, I manage to walk up to him without displaying too many emotions. He places an arm comfortingly around my shoulders, kissing the crown of my head in a decidedly platonic way.

'So, Toby, how do you know the lovely Jane?' simpers Cherry, clearly enjoying the awkwardness of our reunion.

'She's a family friend,' Toby responds abruptly. 'We've known each other a very long time...'

'But never any romantic involvement?'

'No!' I yelp, wanting nothing more than to leave this hideous situation, crawl back home and not open the front door to another living soul for the next year.

'Well, that might all be set to change!' announces Cherry with an accompanying drum roll. 'Because for your blind date, you'll be travelling to...wait for it...oh.' There was a pause as she did a double-take at the contents of the envelope she had opened. Typically, the contestants of this show were sent somewhere warm, sunny and exotic. 'The Isle of Wight?'

Instantly, Toby roars with laughter. Even I can't help but snigger. The location in question is a small island located a very short distance from the south coast of mainland England. Indeed, it is only a stone's throw away from where we were both brought up, in neighbouring Hampshire.

'Perfect!' exclaims Toby, sending me a gleeful look. 'My Nan's in a retirement home there; perhaps we can find the time for a quick visit?'

The production team are clearly very keen to get rid of us, given that we are unquestionably troublemakers who are taking the piss out of their precious show. Toby and I are swiftly bundled into the back of a chauffeur-driven limousine together, along with the suitcases we were advised to bring with us.

'Well...that was fun,' smirks Toby, sending me a sideways glance which agitates the hairs on the back of my neck.

'Yeah, tremendously so,' I reply with abundant sarcasm, before leaning forwards to see what goodies are stored in the on-board refrigerator. If this really is an all-expenses paid few nights away, then I intend to take full advantage of the facilities. Besides, I don't think I'm entirely up to making conversation with the delectable Toby. The most time we've ever spent alone together before today, probably only totals minutes. We are used to others being around us, removing the need for us to converse directly. I'm assuming that's the reason I feel this tongue-tied.

'Hey, come on,' he soothes, elbowing me playfully, as one would do to a sibling. 'Don't be like that, Janie.'

I glance at him questioningly. Janie is the childhood nickname he and Mike always used to call me when I was younger, purely because they knew it annoyed the hell out of me. Fortunately, these days, I remember it rather fondly. Ah! Result! Happily, I locate a good number of those miniature bottles of alcohol you get in hotel rooms. Grabbing a couple of Jack Daniels, I pass one over to Toby before taking a swig of mine, straight from the bottle. The potent liquid hits the back of my throat, causing my eyes to slide closed and I lean back in the seat once more. Better. Maybe if I just get seriously drunk, I can float through the next forty-eight hours, collect my ten thousand pounds, and be on my way.

'I do believe they also supply glasses,' Toby observes, his lips twitching in obvious amusement.

'I'm sure they do...'

'Look, I'm sorry if you think you were my last choice,' he admits with a sigh, running a hand through his immaculate dark hair, in such a way that makes me long to touch it.

'But I was, wasn't I?'

'Yeah, but...' Unusually, he looks uncomfortable. Normally so full of confidence and bravado, it's a side of him that I haven't seen for a long time.

'It's honestly not a problem. I only did it for the money anyway,' I interrupt, lying breezily. From the thoughtful expression on Toby's face, I'm not entirely sure he believes me but he takes a sip of his drink, rather than responding. 'I may not be the girl everybody wants, but at least I'm not the girl that everyone's had.'

For some time, we fly down the motorway, heading towards the south coast, without a further word being shared between us. I'm grateful there is some music playing on the radio, just to drown out the overwhelming sound of silence. In such close proximity, I can't prevent breathing in Toby's scent, immediately reminding me of our shared kiss in the booth. Is it lemon, but also a hint of spice? Whatever he's wearing, it's driving me slightly crazy. I try to breathe through my mouth, as a sensual throbbing commences in my core. Knowing I need to get a handle on myself, I turn away from him slightly and thrust my hands deep in the pockets of my coat. Unexpectedly, I locate my missing car keys. Well, that's just sodding typical. Thanks very much, fate.

I start to wonder whether I haven't always been attracted to Toby; it is kind of difficult not to be. He's the whole package. Not only does he look divine, but he's kind, funny, personable and loyal; I've observed the latter from the long-term and close friendship he's maintained with my brother over the decades. One day, I could only have been about fifteen years old, Toby tried to kiss me on the cheek. My brother went properly ape-shit and nearly strangled him. Needless to say, Toby never considered trying it again. I'm not sure what has suddenly made me think of that memory, when I haven't accessed it for nearly twenty years. But it had been at that moment, I acknowledged Toby was a heartbreaker and that I should keep my distance. If only my adult self-possessed as much sense as when I was a child.

CHAPTER 4

TOBY

After a somewhat awkward car journey to the coast, followed by a short ferry crossing across to the Isle of Wight, Janie and I find ourselves in a surprisingly luxury cottage. Despite it being dark when we arrive, from what I can tell, we are in an idyllic location. Perched high on the cliffs, I can hear the crash of waves far beneath us. If only I possessed a similarly tranquil relationship with the woman I'm sharing this house with, then everything would be perfect. Not only is she rightly pissed off with me, but thanks to having it drummed into my head throughout my entire life that Janie is off limits, I feel like I'm on a romantic few nights away with my kid sister. It just feels wrong. And yet, that kiss we shared keeps returning to the forefront of my memory, stirring a lust from within. I can feel myself starting to grow hard, each and every time I allow it any airtime in the brain.

'What on earth made you agree to this?' I sigh at last. I can't hold my question in any longer. We've been drinking fairly continuously since leaving the production studio and are sprawled out on the sofa, the television providing a welcome degree of background noise.

'I dunno,' she huffs, struggling to sit upright before finishing her glass of red wine. 'I guess part of me just wanted to know.'

I don't dare ask exactly what it was she wanted to know.

'And do you have any answers?' I query, genuinely interested.

'No, just more questions,' she admits, cryptically.

Another subject area which definitely doesn't warrant exploring any further, I silently acknowledge to myself.

'I'm off to bed,' she announces directly. Rising to her feet, she glances nervously down at me. 'Night.'

'Goodnight, Janie,' I sigh, recognising this could well be the longest forty-eight hours of my life.

I hear the click of her bedroom door closing and inhale deeply. Reaching for the remote control, I flick through the channels until I find a decent action movie; always an excellent choice for removing me from the reality of everyday life. Making sure the volume is low enough, so as not to disturb Janie's sleep, I settle back onto the sofa. I know I should get some rest, but ever since I rescued Christie from that river, my sleep patterns have been seriously disturbed. Whenever I close my eyes, I see the swirling brown waters and marvel at the serendipitous timing which allowed me to be in exactly the right location, to observe her coming up for air, for what could well have been the final time.

Recently, I've found numbing my imagination with a film and avoiding sleep is the best way to ensure those still very vivid memories don't entirely swamp my thoughts. Of course, having the media sniffing around on a fairly constant basis doesn't help me move on with my normal, everyday life either. I fervently wish I could return to a time when the motives of those surrounding me could be completely trusted. I abruptly realise that, to some extent, as a trusted family friend, I can do just that with Jane. Maybe I should view these next few days as spending some time with a person who knows me, for the man I truly am.

At some point, I must have drifted off to sleep in front of one of several films I'd been watching. When I wake abruptly, the dimly lit clock in the room informs me it is three in the morning. I gaze around, feeling somewhat startled, wondering why I am unexpectedly awake. Reaching for the remote control, I go to turn the television off, when a whimpering moan catches my attention. Immediately, every sense is on high alert. Muting the volume, I glance around, eyes wide and staring through the gloom. I recognise that the sound is coming from Janie's bedroom. Using the flickering television screen as a guiding light, I tiptoe through the house and hover outside her closed bedroom door.

'Noooooo!' Once again, I hear her anguished moans. Instinct quickly kicks in and I push open the door, adrenaline coursing through me, ready to confront any intruder who might be hurting Janie. But thankfully there is no-one in her room, other than the unwanted intruder within the horrors of the nightmare she is currently having to endure. Her body is twisting from side to side, jaw muscles tight with fear, as she fights off her imaginary attacker.

'Janie,' I murmur softly. Reaching her bedside, I sit down and attempt to squeeze her arms, encouraging her awake. 'Janie!' I urge a little more forcefully, as the nightmare continues.

She awakes with a start, looking fearfully towards me. Her lungs expand dramatically to pull in rapid, gasping breaths. With wide, staring eyes she observes me, as her conscious mind gradually catches up with her imaginary one.

'You were dreaming,' I say, rushing to explain why she should find me perched on the side of her bed in the still of the night.

'I was nightmare-ing,' she moans, scrunching up her face in an attempt to erase the images that are still so real.

'You're okay now. You're safe,' I say soothingly, stroking a strand of hair away from her face.

'Mmm, I know,' she groans sleepily, her eyes starting to flicker closed once more. 'Sleep next to me?'

'I...I...' I don't know how to respond to that.

'Please?' she sighs, reaching for my hand and ineffectually attempting to pull me into her bed, even though she's already half asleep.

'Are you sure?'

'Mmmm, yeah,' she groans in reply.

Experiencing an unexpected surge of heat passing through me, I don't need telling twice. Pulling back the bedcovers, I slide in beside her. After a small amount of jostling, she ends up facing away from me, my arms wrapped around her from behind. Now fully awake myself, I lay there quietly, gently squeezing, trying to provide a safe haven for her to fall back to sleep in.

'Mmmm, that feels so nice,' she admits, releasing a sigh so long, that I marvel whether it will ever end. Leaning her head against my chest, she snuggles back contentedly, her hand sliding up to rest upon my thigh, fingers playfully stroking.

I find myself fully alert to the dangers and feel obliged to advise her of them, even though the last thing I want her to do is stop.

'Janie?'

'Yeah...' she growls sleepily, her fingers continuing to slide against my trouser-clad leg. Every tiny movement she makes is having a powerful effect on me. In less than a minute, I'm rock-hard and feeling as horny as hell.

'I don't know for sure, but there are bound to be some hidden cameras on this property, along with the ones we know about.' We had previously noticed a couple of cameras in plain sight, no doubt there to capture what happens between us, when the camera crew aren't present. 'I don't know if there are any in the bedrooms, but it honestly wouldn't surprise me.' I fear it's that kind of television show.

A pause follows my pronouncement, although it doesn't stop Janie's playful fingers, occasionally causing me to grunt against my will, when she gets incredibly close to where I most want to be touched.

'Perverts,' she mutters after only a short deliberation. I half-chuckle in agreement although the noise ends up sounding more like a muted cry.

'I can't argue with you there. But I really don't want to give them any material.'

'Mmm, good call,' she replies in such a way which suggests she is already on her way back to sleep. 'But nothing will ever happen between us, will it? So you don't need to worry...'

'No?' I query, wondering why not.

'No. I'll always just be a Plain Jane to you...'

I intend to answer. To deny. To explain that nothing could be further from the truth. For although I guiltily recall Mike and I calling her that in our younger years, she is a Plain Jane no longer. Indeed, she has blossomed into a beautiful, intelligent, highly desirable woman. One that I'm finding it increasingly difficult to view as the out of bounds sister of my best mate. After all, we're all adults now. Surely Mike wouldn't have a problem if something were to happen between us, would he? But I'm too late. She's already asleep.

Holding her tight, I continue to stroke Jane's soft, warm skin, revelling in the feel of her. Of being so close to her. I'm still achingly hard; a sensation that fails to leave me for the rest of the night. Even though I know she's asleep, I try not to be too obvious, keeping my hips slightly retracted so that my erection doesn't nestle too much against her ass. Unfortunately, every so often, she sleepily readjusts her position, inadvertently nudging against me. Each time, I try, and fail, to hold in a low grunt.

I wake gradually the following morning, surprised to have slept so well, albeit only for a few hours. Since the incident with Christie, I've been guilty of experiencing a few nightmares of my own, but not last night. I feel refreshed, centred and extremely relaxed. None more so, when I realise that Janie remains fast asleep in my arms, held tightly against my body.

'Hmmmm,' she sighs at last, not sounding in the least concerned that she is waking up with company. 'What are you doing here?'

'You asked me to stay.'

'I did?' she queries, glancing behind to try and ascertain if I'm serious.

'Yes, after you had a nightmare,' I explain.

'Oh. I must be very brave when I'm asleep.'

'You are,' I confirm. A grin spreads across my face at the thrilling memory of how her wandering hands had trailed over my thigh and higher still. 'You're very brave indeed.'

CHAPTER 5

JANE

Something has altered between us. I can't exactly pinpoint when it happened, but it certainly has. As though a bad spell has been broken, I feel much easier in Toby's company and our chatter has barely stopped since we got up. We are currently sitting out on the balcony sharing breakfast, the crash of waves recognisable from far below. The house is so beautiful, it could be a movie setting although, I guess, given our time here is going to be broadcast on television, I suppose it is. Since Toby and I have been getting on so well, I keep forgetting we aren't just here by chance, but for a very specific purpose.

As we briefly sit in companionable silence, sipping the remainder of our tea, a number of vehicles tear noisily up the drive, disturbing our precious peace. The camera crew have arrived.

'And so it begins,' I hear Toby muttering underneath his breath, before looking in my direction. 'Look, I'm sorry about this. I'd much rather we could just enjoy some time together...to catch up,' he quickly clarifies.

'That's okay,' I smile, secretly incredibly touched by his admission. 'I reckon we could probably have some fun with them though, don't you?'

'I very much doubt that!' he scoffs.

'Well, I'm not afraid to wind them up. I'm only here for the cash anyway,' I shrug, in a pathetic attempt to look nonchalant.

'Yeah, sure you are.'

'I am,' I state more firmly, concerned that he understands my motives far too well. Nobody needs to know that, before the ten thousand pounds bribe was mentioned, I was scarcely going to be paid anything. And yet I was still willing to tag along.

'You're not here for the money. You've always been far too pure of heart to lie, Janie. It's one of the things I've always...liked about you,' he finishes, sounding far less self-assured than normal.

'I didn't think you'd ever noticed me,' I confess, not daring to look him in the eyes any longer.

'Oh, I noticed,' admits Toby seriously. 'You're kind of difficult to ignore.'

'That doesn't sound good...'

'It's good, trust me,' Toby instantly replies, just as we are interrupted by company.

'Good morning! I'm Dinah!' the producer exclaims over-enthusiastically, walking across to our table and instantly breaking the mood. She is dressed in bright, almost ostentatious clothing with heavy makeup and pink highlights in her hair. Obviously a morning person, it's difficult to imagine, but she's almost as annoying as Cherry. This kind of program must be a magnet for them. 'Now, this is just perfect! If we set up the camera here, please,' she specifies, barking out orders to her minions. 'And then we'll film you eating breakfast.'

'We've just eaten breakfast,' I retort, not in the best mood after having our tête-à-tête interrupted in this way. Just as it was starting to get interesting too. 'But if you hang on for a couple of hours, you can catch the lunchtime feeding session.'

I hear Toby's deep chuckle beside me and feel buoyed to continue.

'Well...perhaps we can just put some tasty nibbles on the table?' the producer suggests. 'Excuse me, while I go and hunt down something suitable.'

It seems to take forever, as croissants, orange juice, a vase of flowers and all manner of ridiculous paraphernalia are brought out to dress the scene.

'Seriously?' huffs Toby, sending me an unimpressed glance.

'I feel like I should have learnt some lines,' I mutter. 'Do you think we should recite a little Shakespeare?'

'Do you know any off by heart?' asks Toby, looking mildly impressed.

'Er...yeah. I reckon I could summon up that bit in Macbeth about Newt's eyes boiling and baking in a cauldron...'

'I'm not sure that's quite the romantic tone this programme is seeking,' laughed Toby, a faraway look in his eye suggesting a memory outside of the current moment was amusing him.

'What?' I demand, my cheeks hurting from trying not to smile too broadly. I can't help it, but I simply love being in Toby's company. I feel like I'm a kid again; excited, playful, free.

'I've just realised something...on the occasions that your brother and I got into trouble at school, you were often the catalyst....the ringleader.'

'And you've only just worked that out?' I tease in mock astonishment. 'Bit slow, aren't you?'

'Yeah, I am,' agrees Toby. He's suddenly looking at me in a very curious way, which is making my tummy fizz and my brain feel cold. 'I've been incredibly slow.'

I get the distinct impression there might be a double-meaning to his words, but before I build up the courage to quiz him on this, Dinah has returned.

Ironically, by the time they've finished filming us over our fake breakfast, it is *actually* lunchtime.

'So, we've got a challenge for the two of you now,' she announces with unnecessary hype. Toby and I share a subtle look and I feel like I'm back at school, secretly displaying my aversion for an irritating teacher. I watch Toby's eyes crinkle at the corners when he reads the meaning behind my expression and, instantly, my heart warms. Is it my imagination, or is he smiling way more than any of the other times I've seen him over the years. Perhaps he's just grateful to be sharing this experience with a friend he can trust, instead of a psycho that he can't.

'A five mile hike of the surrounding area,' Dinah continues valiantly, given that neither of us have provided any obvious feedback that we're interested in what she's saying.

'Cool,' I smile. 'With the camera crew?'

'Of course,' she confirms, looking puzzled at my suggestion, subtly reminding me that obtaining juicy snippets for their precious programme is the only reason we are all here.

'Great! Let's do it!' exclaimed Toby, obviously reading my mind. We are both pretty fit and the camera crew look decidedly less so. If we can't outrun them entirely, we can at least have fun trying.

THE FIRST COUPLE of miles of our alleged hike go off without a hitch. Although, of course, it really isn't a hike. There is nothing taxing about the route we are taking which comprises wide, peaceful tracks through glorious countryside, delightful vistas and precious little sign of a gradient to challenge us. Over time, via an unspoken agreement, we intensify the pace just prior to a wide, sweeping corner in the path ahead. As we move out of their sight, fleetingly unsupervised, Toby takes my hand in his own larger one. The sensation of his skin on mine is warm and soft, promptly sending a zing of excitement along my arm before dissipating throughout the remainder of my trembling form.

'Come on,' he urges, the naughtiest smile I have ever seen, plastered across his handsome face. 'Run!'

With a rush of elation, I do just that, following him willingly into the thick foliage towards goodness only knows where. After about only ten seconds, he pulls me down to squat in the undergrowth, behind the wide, gnarled trunk of an ancient Oak. As we hide in silence, waiting for our chaperones to realise they have lost us, I place a hand over my mouth in an attempt not to laugh. Toby squeezes my hand and my eyes slide mischievously to his, only to discover my amusement is instantly dampened. The look in his eyes all but takes my breath away; determined, passionate and extremely telling, I automatically retract my gaze, afraid of what he is silently trying to disclose.

'This way,' he murmurs unexpectedly, and I find myself being led further away from the direction in which the camera crew have headed.

For a short while, we walk in silence until we reach a great expanse of deserted coastline. The shore is low-lying here, waves gently and rhythmically lapping up the sand. It is extremely peaceful and I inhale the salty air deeply as Toby leads us towards a small wooden pontoon with boats moored along its length.

'Please don't imagine I'm going swimming with you!' I warn jokingly, as we scramble onto the pontoon and it wobbles alarmingly.

'Don't you trust me?' he challenges, an eyebrow raised questioningly. Is it wrong that I just want to consume that eyebrow, and the rest of him, then and there?

'Strangely, I do,' I admit, receiving a wink in return, which does all manner of bad things to my body and fails to dampen my ardour.

'Come on then.'

Having identified a suitable sailing boat, Toby quickly unzips the canvas cover and we both disappear inside. Making our way towards the dusty windows at the front, we bend low so as not to be seen, sniggering at the sight of our minders still searching for us. We are well aware that Dinah will be pissed but strangely, that just makes me relish the moment even more.

'I reckon if we lay low here for a while, it won't take them long to give up,' explains Toby, taking a seat on a long cushioned bench that follows the curve of the boat. 'Then we've got the rest of the day to ourselves.'

'Sounds like a plan,' I confirm, sitting close by, a grin lighting up my face. 'And what do you intend on doing with this unexpected free time? Visit your nan perhaps?'

'Unlikely,' he replies, faintly amused. 'She's on the other side of the island.'

'Ah, shame,' I pretend to sympathise, the sarcasm in my tone undeniable. 'Maybe tomorrow?' Toby observes me thoughtfully.

'You know, that cheeky streak of yours might get you into trouble one of these days.'

'What kind of trouble?' I enquire, inhaling sharply. Watching his eyes narrow as he studies me carefully, I know *exactly* what kind of trouble I'd like to be in right now. For the longest time, Toby doesn't respond. Instead, we sit there in silence, the pressure building. The boat rocks gently with the light wind and the only sound is the echoing, metallic chime of rigging lines tapping against the mast.

'H...how long do you think we should stay here?' I stutter, feeling disarmed by his silence, his gaze, his intensity. *Forever*, my mind instantly supplies as an answer. Please say forever. Because the fact of the matter is, right now, I don't want to be anywhere else in the world, but beside this glorious man.

CHAPTER 6

TOBY

'Well, I guess that entirely depends,' I answer at last. Is it crazy that I can sense the air literally crackling around us with static electricity?

'On what?' Janie queries. I observe her chewing her bottom lip in anticipation of my answer and I find myself mesmerised. Drowning in desire, I realise with a jolt that I need to experience one of her kisses again. The first one was so damn good. I physically crave Mike's little sister. Is that wrong? Maybe. Right now, do I care? Probably not. Certainly not enough to practice any form of self-control.

'Hey!' she calls, quickly returning my attention to the room.

'Huh? What?'

'Are you purposefully trying to make me feel uneasy, leaving these long gaps in our conversations?'

'No,' I reply immediately. Janie doesn't need to be told the real reason behind my pauses; that she overwhelms my mind and prevents me from thinking straight. 'Why, is it working?' I add with a chuckle, knowing full well that my question will get a rise.

'You arse!' she moans, responding with a playful shove to my shoulder. But I'm ready for her. I know her from old. Unexpectedly capturing her hand in mine, I hold it against my chest, stroking gently. In silence, I study her closely. Heat has already rushed to her cheeks which are reddening under my continued scrutiny. She shifts slightly uncomfortably in her chair, as though trying to find a better position. Inhaling through her mouth now, her breaths are shorter and more rapid.

'It entirely depends on what you want to do while you're here,' I admit. The instant I've spoken, I hold my breath, able to feel a quilt of muscles dance across my jaw as I uneasily clench my teeth together. There. I've said it. And it's no small question that's been laid on the line. The answer potentially impacts the long-term friendship I have with one of my best mates, for a start.

'Did you have anything specific in mind?' she answers cautiously. We are both progressing with baby-steps, knowing that one false move might screw up the relaxed friendship we have managed to successfully build.

'Well...' I begin, ready to bite the bullet. 'You know that kiss we shared?'

'Uh-huh,' confirms Janie, her eyes flicking towards my mouth and then away once more.

'I did kinda enjoy it.'

'Only *kinda*?' she objects.

'I *really* enjoyed it,' I admit, unable to prevent myself grinning at the sight of her face, which is a mixture of amusement and mock indignation.

'Yeah?'

'Yeah,' I confirm assertively. 'Want to try it again though, just to be sure?'

'That sounds like a phenomenally bad idea,' she breathes.

'Mmmm, doesn't it.' Pulling her towards me, I encourage Janie to straddle my lap. As my muscled thighs take her weight, I glance up, the intensity in our stare almost too much to handle.

'Let's not forget the last time we kissed,' she warned, her breathing now little more than fast, shallow panting. I have no doubt in my mind that she wants me equally as much as I want her. Which is a pretty amazing feeling, given how much I hunger for her right now. 'You rejected me and chose another woman.'

'I didn't reject *you* personally,' I assure her. 'I rejected Miss Past, on the understanding that she must have been an ex of mine. I can guarantee, I will never reject you, Janie Green. And I would never knowingly hurt you.'

'Toby...' she starts to stutter. I've no doubt that she's about to suggest why this isn't the best idea. But I don't agree.

'It's a wonder I didn't do this years ago,' I sigh, reaching up to cup her delicate jaw. And then we gradually draw closer, as though controlled by an invisible force which makes our joining together inevitable. With infinite tenderness, our lips combine; slowly exploring, testing, teasing. Our mouths fully engaged, we enjoy an intense conversation that renders words superfluous. On and on we continue, marvelling at the simple act of kissing, combined with stroking hands which lovingly echo our unspoken desires.

But the burning passion that we each have for each other, can only be suppressed for so long. Our hands are soon exploring more thoroughly. My lips eventually break away from Janie's mouth, wandering temptingly down her neck, making her moan shamelessly as she subtly grinds her pelvis against me. Feeling as hard as iron myself, her actions are not helpful, causing the ache inside me to become unbearable.

Growling with frustrated need, I swiftly reposition us, laying Janie down on the long padded seat before taking my place above. As my mouth returns to hers, the fire builds significantly with our altered position. I allow my weight to pin her down as she writhes in response. Instantly, she moans wantonly into my mouth, the vibrations of her voice setting my body alight. Apparently, Janie is extremely amenable to being trapped firmly beneath me, allowing me to take control of our pleasure and deal with her in my own slow, sweet time.

FUCK. Things are starting to get out of control. I might have lied to myself that I'm capable of taking this slowly, because I literally can't keep my hands off her. Both partially undressed now, my fingers are teasing and tickling across Janie's tummy as she rolls her hips lustfully. Occasionally my fingers dip under the waistband of her panties, resulting in a pained, frustrated cry, as she is reminded of exactly what I want to give her. Exactly what I want to do to her. I know she's equally as turned on as I am. She may still be dressed...just...but I can smell her arousal. I can only imagine how swollen and wet her pussy is. How good she will taste. I break our kiss and swallow once again, as my mouth naturally salivates in response to the thought. My lips fall to her neck, her collar bone, her chest... I know I've *got* to stop kissing this glorious woman. It's just practically impossible to achieve. Fuck it. Reluctantly, I pull back.

'Jesus!' Janie gasps, gazing up at me in awe. 'Have you ever felt anything like that?'

'Never...' I admit, trying to control my breathing. And as much as I want to suggest we continue and damn the consequences, I simply can't allow it. 'But we probably ought to stop.'

'Why?' My heart lurches to see her suddenly looking so forlorn, as though I'm about to reject her in some way. Tell her it's all been a horrible mistake.

'Because I'm struggling to trust myself with you,' I admit honestly, tenderly stroking her face, trying to remove the obvious hurt. 'And the more we allow to happen now, the more impossible it will be for me to keep my hands off you later.'

'You want to keep your hands off me?'

'For now, yes,' I state firmly. 'We've got another twenty-four hours under the watchful eyes of the *Blast from the Past* team. I refuse to give them any material. Whatever happens between us is private, and that's how it will always be.'

I have a powerful urge to protect Janie, so this is non-negotiable. And I don't just mean protecting her honour and her reputation, but I'm also concerned about the crazy people that are attracted towards an alleged *celebrity*, as well as their family and friends. Just take the other two contestants on the show, as a prime example. This short time spent with Janie has made me realise more than ever, how I only want to surround myself with real, honest, true people moving forwards.

'And our first time is not going to be here,' I add, before she attempts to encourage me down a path of thinking that will undoubtedly uncover my weakness for her.

'So, you're planning on there being a first time, are you?' she teases, the sparkle returning to her eyes, once she understands the reasoning behind my apparent rejection.

'Trust me, there *will* be a first time,' I confirm, dropping my lips briefly onto hers. 'And a second,' I add, before kissing her once again. 'And a third...and a fourth...and a fifth,' I add, kissing her each time. And a hundredth, and a thousand if I get my way, I don't say out loud.

'Okay! Okay! I get it! There will be a lot of shagging,' she giggles, her hand sliding temptingly over my ass. 'Although truthfully, I'm not sure I can hold off until we get back home.'

'We're only here for another day or so,' I explain, in what is hopefully a soothing tone. 'Then we're free to do as we please.'

'Twenty-four hours living under the same roof with someone I desire more than oxygen?' queries Janie sarcastically. 'Mmmmm, yeah. That should be easy.'

Of course, Janie raises an excellent point. After experiencing such an overload of pleasure, albeit for the briefest moment, it is almost impossible to fight the desire I have to undertake a repeat performance. Back at the house, we find ourselves once more surrounded on all sides by hidden cameras, along with an irate television producer, livid that we managed to give her camera crew the slip for the better part of three hours. And even worse, that we are apparently unable to provide an adequate explanation for exactly what went on during our unanticipated absence. Regrettably, the excuse that we just got lost isn't fooling anyone.

CHAPTER 7

TOBY

'Stop ogling,' I mutter under my breath, as Janie walks past me in the kitchen. I just hope the microphones aren't sensitive enough to pick up what I said, but either way, it's worth it for the astonished look I receive in return. She can try and deny it as much as she likes, but I know full well that she's subtly watching me the entire time, just as I'm aware of every move she makes. It's a very strange and frustrating situation, to be physically burning with desire for someone, who has admitted they are equally attracted to you, but unable to do a damn thing about it.

'Toby!' comes a shriek from a nearby room, swiftly rousing me from my deliberations.

'What is it?' I shout, quickly heading towards Janie's voice.

'There's a spider behind the door of the toilet!' she exclaims, in a girlish voice that doesn't sound like her at all. 'Please help me!'

'Okay,' I agree, feeling somewhat perplexed. I've suffered my fair share of partners who are more concerned with their nails or general appearance than what truly matters in life. In comparison, Janie is active, practical, modest and apparently unafraid. Put simply, I've never known anyone else like her. So, out of all the women I've known, I'd have thought she is the least likely to be concerned with a spider. Cautiously pushing open the door to the bathroom, I encounter a most unusual sight. Janie is standing on top of the toilet seat, pointing in horror at an apparently marauding arachnid.

'You'll have to close the door!' instructs Janie. 'Quick! Before it moves again!'

Following her instructions, I do as she requests, sealing us inside the small room. But, all that is visible are clean, white-washed walls.

'Hey,' she murmurs seductively. I turn to face her, feeling beyond confused. Suddenly, she leaps from the toilet against my body, wrapping her legs firmly around my waist. 'You've got exactly one minute before we start to raise suspicions,' she purrs into my ear. 'Make the most of it.'

I don't need telling twice. With a low groan of desire, I back Janie up against the wall, trapping her firmly in place. Naturally, my mouth clashes against hers; plundering, ravaging, possessing, taking what is mine. Our tongues entwine, causing us to jointly moan out our desires and frustrations, of which we have plenty.

'How long have we got?' I growl, as my mouth breaks away from hers and starts nipping down her soft neck, causing all manner of gasps and squeaks that I don't mind admitting I am quickly becoming addicted to. I can't help but admire her inspired move; there might be hidden cameras elsewhere in the house, but in the bathroom, not only would their presence be hugely depraved, but also illegal. This might be our only safe space in the entire house.

'Out of time,' she admits, sounding as disappointed as I feel.

'You don't even know how lovely you are, do you?' I sigh, gazing at her longingly. Then I place her gently back to the ground, kiss her on the forehead and turn for the exit.

'It's a big one, isn't it?' she shrieks, just as I turn the handle. Immediately, I am forced to quickly close the door as I dissolve into hysterical laughter beside this amazing woman, who is responsible for bringing cheer and optimism back into my life. It takes a little time before I've composed my facial expressions sufficiently enough to return.

'Yeah,' I manage to agree at last. 'It's a really big one. And it's all yours after tomorrow.' Then I walk out of the room, a hero in the eyes of the viewers of *Celebrity Blast from the Past* for having successfully dealt with the spider that never was.

I'M WATCHING Janie in amusement. She's currently making various trips between the house and balcony which overlooks the sea, apparently in preparation for our evening meal. The food is already warming in the oven. Janie has laid the table, using what is simply the most enormous tablecloth I have ever seen. No matter what she does with it, it trails the ground like an oversized curtain.

'Stop perving,' she mutters under her breath, passing by next to me on her way back into the kitchen.

'Not a chance,' I chuckle in reply. After all, she's a gorgeous woman and I'm male, horny and wanting to be hers. What the hell does she expect?

I probably should have guessed her scheming plan, but over dinner, I quickly discover that the choice of tablecloth was not made by chance. Indeed, it was very purposefully selected, for it completely blocks out everything that takes place beneath the table from the cameras. Almost the instant I sit down, I'm aware of Janie's foot starting to trail temptingly up my thigh, nudging against my almost unbearably thick erection, teasing me as much as she dares. For a short while, I do my best to disregard quite how much she is turning me on, but I am hard and throbbing. The situation is swiftly becoming untenable. Subtly, I drop a hand to my lap, firmly wrapping my fingers around Janie's slender ankle to capture her.

'What exactly do you think you're doing?' I murmur under my breath.

'Turning you on?' she suggests impishly, looking disproportionately pleased with herself. Something I feel obliged to rectify.

Still holding her ankle tightly, I lower my other hand and start to stroke the base of her stockinged foot with my fingers. Across the table, I can see the effect I'm having on her. Clearly ticklish and undeniably aroused, I watch with pleasure as Janie's face reddens. Her perfect body is being forced to subtly twist and grind on the chair as she tries, in vain, to escape me. I can imagine her pussy inevitably reacting, the muscles clamping down as arousal gathers. Just the thought of it makes me harder than ever. Deciding that Janie hasn't suffered enough yet, I progress to rubbing her foot against my thick, swollen cock, to ensure she knows exactly what awaits her. For the sake of the cameras, both of us are trying our best not to react to the wicked deed I'm continuing to undertake, but it's almost impossible. Eventually, I release her, before leaning forwards to share some suitable thoughts on her behaviour.

'Please don't think I'll forget this. Or that I won't take my revenge at a more convenient time.'

The rest of the evening continues in much the same manner, getting what little interaction we can, when we can. We finish the night watching a film on the sofa, enjoying what I hope will look like a platonic cuddle to the viewers at home but in reality, is anything but. In the form of low murmurs, private thoughts are shared as scorching hot looks inform the other of our true intentions.

The backs of Janie's fingers start to very innocently stroke my abdomen as she hugs me, her touch very gradually wandering further down. I have an urge to lift her into my arms with a roar, march into the bedroom and devour every inch of her.

'Don't test me,' I murmur quietly into her ear. Even to me, I sound like a man on the absolute edge. Janie wriggles herself around slightly, our faces now just inches from each other. I can feel her soft breath floating across my mouth, only increasing the hunger I feel.

'Can you sleep with me, like last night?' she mutters, a hopeful look in her eyes. 'I can pretend to have another nightmare.'

'No,' I huff, shaking my head brusquely. 'There's no way I'll be able to keep my hands off you, even though I know there might be cameras. There's no point pretending that I can.'

'Oh! This is unbearable!' she exclaims, temporarily forgetting we are surrounded by cameras. 'Fucking pervs!'

I have to agree. It is a little disconcerting that every move we make will potentially be shared with a nationwide audience.

'It's only until tomorrow,' I try to sooth, able to feel Janie trembling beneath my touch as I stroke her back. Having her cuddled against me, holding, caressing, adoring. Well, it all feels incredibly comforting.

'Seriously, I don't think I can bear this,' she groans. 'You have no idea how horny I feel.'

'I do, believe me,' I sigh. Because I feel exactly the same. 'Look, let's just go to bed...separately,' I clarify. 'Then when we wake up, we'll only have a few hours to wait.'

Following my suggestion, we go to bed shortly afterwards and I'm surprised to discover that I fall asleep pretty fast. I don't wake up until early dawn. The light is just starting to creep under the bottom of the curtains and my phone is beeping, to signify I've received a number of text messages, all of which are from Janie.

'Seriously, I can't bear this any longer,' states the most recent one, sent only three minutes ago. Immediately, I feel blood pump to my already semi-erect cock and instantly, I'm horny again.

'Leave it with me,' I reply. Fuck only knows what I'm going to do, but I get out of bed and head towards the bathroom. There, inspiration strikes me. Turning both of the bath taps onto full power, I walk back out of the room, heading into the kitchen to make myself a cup of tea. Returning ten minutes later, I'm unsurprised to discover the room is completely flooded.

'Oh shit!' I groan, holding my hand dramatically over my mouth.

'What's happening?' demands Janie, pulling open her bedroom door and glancing at me in shock. For a flash, I can't speak. I am too busy drinking in my first sight of her on this new day.

'Bathroom's flooded,' I admit, wading across the saturated floor to turn off the taps. 'I went to make myself a cup of tea, forgetting that I'd left the bath running.'

'Well, that was very silly of you,' she said, in a voice that sounded reproachful, although her eyes were telling quite a different story. They were sparkling with excited, hopeful delight.

'Grab your stuff while I call a cab. I saw a hotel a couple of miles down the road. We'll book into a room there, so we can get freshened up, before we return to the house later this morning.'

'Oh...what a nuisance,' complained Janie, trying not to smile as she returned to her bedroom and shut the door. 'I was having a really good sleep too.' Ten seconds later, I receive another text.

'You are my absolute hero,' it says. 'Please consider how you'd like me to reward you?'

CHAPTER 8

JANIE

'Fuck me,' I daringly request, as the hotel door closes behind us and we are completely alone at last. I feel my tummy roll with lust, as Toby steps forwards and takes me decisively into his arms.

'It's half past six,' Toby groans, kissing from my forehead down to my nose. 'Dinah's made it pretty clear we have to be back at the house by nine, ready for filming.'

'So?'

'So, Little Miss Demanding. I am not going to *fuck you*, as you so eloquently put it, if we barely have two hours together. That is simply not happening.'

'What did you have in mind then?' I groan. Surely, the whole point of this elaborate act, was to give us some time together to do just that. 'Game of tiddlywinks?'

'For a start, we aren't going to waste a single minute,' he explains, cupping his hands tenderly around my face and sending a jet of goosebumps clattering down my arms. 'But we aren't going to rush either. No way am I risking the first time we make love being interrupted,' he adds seriously.

'Making love, huh?' I tease, unexpectedly experiencing the

strangest warming sensation spreading through me. I have an urge to give this man everything; every part of me. At this moment, I am his.

'I think so, don't you?' And then he kisses me; slowly, passionately, meaningfully. As our kiss develops, my fingers can't help but explore, loosening any clothing I come into contact with, running my hands pleasurably across Toby's exceptional body. When we eventually pull apart, my pulse is heavy, my pussy is tingling and neither of us have much clothing remaining.

'Oh God,' groans Toby, nipping along my shoulders as he pushes away my unbuttoned blouse. 'How come you're so edible?'

'Just luck, I guess,' I gasp, knowing I'm anything but.

'Come into the shower with me?' he offers with a cheeky glance of his incredible blue eyes, leading me by the hand into the adjoining room.

While the running water heats up, I assist Toby out of the remainder of his clothes, finding myself short of breath. I mean, I always knew he was a seriously attractive guy, but up close, Toby Jacobs is like nothing on this earth. We enjoy a steamy shower, intimately pressed up against each other. My wet, lathered hands joyously revel in every inch of his taut stomach, firm ass, muscled chest and the tastiest looking cock it has ever been my privilege to encounter. Each time I hold Toby intimately and hear that long, low moan of pleasure escaping from his lips, I find myself unable to open my eyes. The overwhelming sense of lust that passes through me, simply becomes too much to bear.

Somehow, we manage to dry ourselves and return to our room, where we collapse onto the bed, kissing deeply. Both equally ravenous, our mouths and hands explore each other's naked bodies.

'Jeez!' Toby growls, as I manage to wriggle out of his embrace and traverse down his body, using the narrow line of hair on his tummy to direct me due south. 'No way can I hide my true feelings for you after this...'

'No?' I query. With my mouth hovering above his throbbing cock, I gaze up wantonly into his eyes, my own voice croaky with emotion. 'What feelings are those, then?'

'Probably the same as yours,' he admits, his statement being broken by a grunt half way through, as my lips drop tenderly onto the tip of his bulbous head. 'Lust...want....desire...hunger...astonishing hunger.'

With a moan of the greed to which he is undoubtedly referring, I ensure Toby is incapable of speaking for quite some time. My hand and mouth work in synchronisation with each other, rejoicing in the pleasure I am able to provide the man I adore, simply from a flick of my tongue, or a gently rocking hand.

'God! You're something else!' Toby grunts, his fingers twisting through my hair, gently assisting with the rhythm, helping me to discover what he needs.

Gradually, I gain confidence, my hands fondling his balls, creeping even further back to trail around his tightly clenched ass. Each time my finger makes contact, not only does Toby's volume increase but I can taste pre-cum leaking onto my taste buds. I'm engulfed with a thrill, knowing how much fun we will have together. He has truly become my drug of choice.

'Janie, I'm so close,' he mutters. I can sense despair in his voice; torn between wanting to come and knowing he hasn't yet provided me with a similar high. But I don't want him to resist. If we aren't going to have sex here, and I do understand his argument for holding back, then I still want to feel him come inside me. Without releasing him from my mouth, I groan, hands around his ass, pulling him further into me, as I silently communicate my desires.

'Oh God!' he groans, as he realises what wickedness I'm wordlessly suggesting. Increasing the speed, Toby gently rocks his hips forwards, matching me for pace, as we both work hard to drive him way beyond the boundaries of his self-control. Heady with lust, I feel his cock swell in my mouth and know he is incredibly close. His breathing accelerates; short, sharp breaths, accompanied by all manner of the most incredible sounds I simply want to experience over and over and over again. And then his hand adjusts around the back of my head, his torso constricts and a long, low growl of ecstasy fills my ears. As he ejaculates straight down the back of my throat, I pull him even closer against me. It feels, in that moment, as though we are one.

'Jesus! Oh fuck!' exclaims Toby, hips still flinching as the last of his release spills into me. Panting hard, he gently retracts from my mouth as my tongue slides loving across his wet skin, eager to ensure I haven't missed a drop. 'God! You are in some trouble now!'

'I am?' I gasp, feeling lightheaded. My body has started to tremble from the sheer intensity. I feel like I've just landed from a parachute jump and immediately, I want to ride it again.

'You are,' he confirms, encouraging my face back onto a level with his. 'Get up here.'

I soon discover that Toby's tender mouth and gently stroking hands are one hell of a lethal combination. Every teasing sweep of his fingers, swipe of his tongue or light nibble from his teeth increasingly fills me with an untamed desire that I fear will soon explode from me. Pushing my legs wide open, he eventually moves into position, balanced above my swollen pussy, making me feel vulnerable, wanton, daring and exposed. Way beyond words now, he has turned me into a desperate, gibbering wreck, as I await his first magical touch.

I am not disappointed. The instant his mouth brushes my swollen lips, dipping fleetingly into the pool of arousal he has been entirely responsible for creating, I know I'm in the hands of an expert. My hips twitch and roll, as an uncontained roar escapes from my throat, so powerful that it causes actual, physical pain.

'You taste amazing,' he groans, before hastily returning his mouth for more.

As Toby's hand joins his mouth in a bid to increase my pleasure, I can sense my internal muscles tightly clenching and releasing, in preparation to accept him. That first stroke of his softly stroking finger offers up so much promise.

'Shhhhh,' he murmurs, as I emit a broken whimper. Ever so slowly, the tip of his finger follows a slippery, unerring path inside; stretching me, thrilling me, touching me so incredibly deep inside.

Feeling lightheaded, my eyes are continually fluttering closed, before I'm forced to glance down at him again in disbelief, wondering what the hell he can be doing, to make me feel so good. Maintaining a steady rhythm, I'm soon aware of Toby's lone finger being joined by a second, before tunnelling back inside. Simultaneously, he curls those wicked fingers slightly and begins to pummel more deeply, making my abdomen clamp down hard. Bolts of pleasure radiate out from my core, hips starting to twist and spasm outside of my control.

'Oh God!' I bellow, for his mouth has now joined in the fray. With his fingers still thrusting inside me, I sense both his mouth and another finger have started to manipulate my pulsing, over-sensitive clit. I literally have no idea what he is doing, but I do know that he is delivering a magnitude of pleasure, the likes of which I have never before known. Now utterly incapable of speech, I emit a range of indecipherable, joyous sounds that dance through the air and encourage Toby not to stop.

In next to no time, a hidden force pulses through me, causing every muscle to stiffen. From out of nowhere, a huge explosion of energy erupts from within, making my hips twist in ecstasy. I am screaming out my release; pleading, clawing, panting, collapsing. My throat is on fire with the force of my exclamation, strong muscles clamping hard around his fingers, moving up and down in waves, pulling him deeper and deeper inside with every grind and twist of my body. To his considerable credit, Toby allows me to ride my mammoth climax without ever once stopping, pushing me through the wet heat and blissful contractions, until every last drop of my desire has been accounted for.

'So, *so* sexy,' he sighs at last, his fingers still resting inside me, his incredibly talented mouth kissing up to tease my throbbing breasts. I can't speak. I can't think. I can't believe it when his hand starts to move again. During that short, magical time we have in private together, Toby proves himself to be an incredibly talented and attentive lover. And I prove myself to be nowhere near as fit as I thought I was. We clearly need to have a lot more practice, to really build up my stamina.

'Janie, listen to me?' he says, after I've experienced so much pleasure, I can scarcely breathe.

'Uh-huh,' I gasp, a shaking bundle of desire in his arms.

'The only reason...and I mean the *only* reason I am letting you rest, is because we're running out of time.'

'We are,' I sigh, a broad smile slowly spreading across my face as I become aware of just how hard he has once more become. 'And right now, I simply don't care...' And with that statement left hanging in the air, I wriggle back down, taking him lovingly into my trembling mouth.

'Later tonight,' grunts Toby, gazing lustfully into my eyes. 'I'm gonna fuck you so good, you'll never want anyone but me, ever again.'

Little does he know, I'm already there. Tonight literally can't arrive fast enough.

CHAPTER 9

TOBY

For the rest of that day, my mind is alive with nothing but Janie and the incredible bond we have discovered within each other. Dinah fails to hide her displeasure when we return to the cottage much later than scheduled. However, each one of her frowns and tuts is more than worth it because I know the reason for our tardiness. I was enjoying the most intense connection that I have ever known, with the most incredible woman I have ever met. And from her wide-eyed, stunned reaction, along with the massive smile she sends me every time our eyes meet, I'm pretty confident that Janie feels exactly the same way.

Throughout the long, tedious hours that precede being released from our contract with the production company, I periodically find myself becoming hard, as memories of the pleasure Janie gave me earlier that morning, burst into my mind. The softness of her mouth, the sureness of her hand, the playful, teasing way she held me on the edge, despite knowing we were horribly late, making me question whether she was even going to permit me to release a second time. But the day is not a wasted one. After all, I am spending it in Janie's company; this amazing woman I have known for the larger part of my life, but have never truly seen before now. Shame on me. For a moment, I regret all the wasted years, where I've messed around with women so thoroughly incapable of meeting my needs and, no doubt, vice versa. And all the time, my perfect partner was staring me right in the face, in the guise of my best friend's sister. At least we've found each other now, though, and I intend to do everything I can to ensure our incredible connection blooms into a long-term partnership.

Once we've been transported back to the recording studio in London, we enter into a sequence of torturously time-consuming takes, retakes and re-retakes with the tedious Cherry. Having apparently forgotten my former rejection of her not so subtle advances at our earlier meeting, Cherry is making fresh attempts to advertise her interest. A squeeze of my bicep here, a stroke of my thigh there. Her frankly disappointing behaviour is a timely reminder of the significance of the growing partnership that Janie and I have found.

Gritting my teeth, I say nothing. Instead, I cast a glance towards Janie, hoping for her silent moral support. She shares a small smile with me, but I see something lurking behind her eyes; a concern, a previously unacknowledged fear that I might not be trustworthy. That I might not seriously value what is growing between us, quite as much as she does. I'm aware I had a reputation, but I've changed over the years. I make a mental note to ensure I explain this to her very soon. I am not the boy I once was; I have grown into a man now. A man who knows exactly what he wants, and the level of trust required to keep it safe.

I breathe an internal sigh of relief, as Cherry asks her final set of questions. Janie and I are almost free. Free to explore the true feelings we have for each other, away from the watchful eye of the media. As our comments are captured and our reactions are recorded, I feel no guilt when the crew believe our mistruths. For neither Janie nor I are willing to share very much on a television programme to be broadcast to millions. For now, the secret we guard is ours, and ours alone.

Leaving the recording studio and walking down the corridor back to our dressing rooms, I am amazed to find myself and Janie completely unchaperoned.

'Still want to finish what we started at the hotel?' I query, feeling slightly unsure of Janie's wishes, since the incident with Cherry's wandering hands.

'Of course,' she mutters. 'Don't you?'

'More than anything,' I admit. 'I reckon my home is about thirty miles closer than yours. Shall I text you the address?' Biting her lip, Janie nods shyly. 'And just for the record,' I add seriously. 'You are the only woman I see and the only woman I want.' I'm warmed by the smile that spreads across her face. It is completely infectious and within seconds we are both grinning inanely at each other.

'You make me so happy,' she admits gruffly.

'Ditto,' I reply. And it's true. I don't remember ever feeling this way before; weightless, excited, hopeful, loved.

Alone in my dressing room, I quickly type out a text to Janie and then read it back through five times, just to be sure I've got every part of my address correct. I don't want a single thing to delay our meeting. I don't see Janie again as I leave the building, although her car is still in situ. Not wanting my desire to be too obvious in front of the prying eyes of the production team, against my better judgement, I drive away. Besides, I know she was asked to speak to the finance team, prior to her departure, to sort out the payment I unknowingly negotiated for her.

I speed home, feeling like a child escaping from school for the summer holidays, free from the shackles which have previously weighed me down. Huge swathes of time stretch out ahead of us, in which I plan to have a lot of fun with Janie and allow us to get to know each other even better. The unanswered question of how we tell her brother of this latest development, hovers uncomfortably in my thoughts, before I push him firmly out of my mind. We will deal with Mike, as and when we are ready. But right now is a time for us, not for worrying about the reaction of our wider families.

The instant I arrive home later that evening, I scurry around turning on heating, picking up post, drawing curtains on the encroaching darkness and trying to make the environment as comfortable as possible for when Janie arrives. At last I hear the doorbell ring and I'm surprised to feel nervous, excited, yet apprehensive.

After all, this is the first time Janie will be seeing the real me. The person I am at home, in private.

I needn't have worried. The moment the front door closes firmly behind her, Janie falls into my arms and we kiss intimately. Not only is it special to have her here in my home, but it's thrilling to sense all the desire and need we have for each other. When we finally break apart, panting deeply, I take her gently by the hand and lead her to my bedroom. As we ascend the stairs, I'm fully aware of my significant erection and offer up a silent nod of thanks that I've already climaxed twice, earlier this morning. There is no question I want to do so again, this time as deep inside Janie as it is physically possible to be. But hopefully I will be able to take my slow, sweet time exploring her body properly, without being haunted by a frantic urgency to come.

'I've missed you,' I breathe, as we collapse onto my huge double bed, our hands naturally falling to each other's bodies, as though inevitably drawn together.

'You only saw me about two hours ago,' she smiles shyly, gazing up at me in a way that sets my heart alight.

'Yeah,' I reply gruffly. 'And that's about an hour and fifty-nine minutes too long to have waited.'

'So impatient...'

'Where you're concerned, yes,' I admit. Apparently unable to prevent myself, my fingers have dropped to her clothing, methodically unfastening zips, buttons and hooks in a bid to be closely united once more. There is simply nothing like the sensation of being pressed up hard against Janie's warm, naked skin, hearing her soft moans in my ear. It's an experience I'm keen to enjoy over and over again.

As my large hands run over her delicate form, appreciating every line and curve, despite our joint pleasure that morning, it still feels as though I'm touching her for the very first time.

'I'm such an idiot to have allowed you to escape me for so long,' I huff. 'You are completely amazing.'

'That's okay,' she grunts, as my fingers tease around her inner thighs, edging closer and closer to the pool of arousal I instinctively know is already waiting for me to explore. 'You've fixed your mistake now. Just be sure not to mess up again.'

'No chance of that,' I sigh, sliding my fingers pleasurably through her swollen mess and revelling in Janie's quiet, breathy groans. 'You're stuck with me, my love.' And what's more, I absolutely mean it.

CHAPTER 10

JANIE

I'm not sure exactly what I was expecting, but it wasn't this. Toby is beyond tender, taking so much time just stroking my body, relaxing me, luxuriating in the feel of my skin and revelling in our combined adulation. I'm hyperaware of his heavy length resting against my trembling thigh, yet all the time he is muttering endearments against my neck, making me believe I'm the most special woman in the world. As a result, I'm so incredibly aroused that it feels like I'm balanced on a knife edge; as though the smallest touch might put me in danger of falling into the pleasurable abyss. And yet that moment is never experienced. Instead, we are left to wallow in our combined longing.

Toby releases an aching nipple from his talented mouth, causing me to yelp with frustration. All the while, his thumb has been leaning against, but not satisfactorily stimulating, my throbbing clit. Try as I might to rotate my hips against him, to drive myself over the edge, Toby is not apparently willing to permit it.

'Please...please...please let me come,' I implore. My skin is trembling, heart racing, legs shaking almost out of control. My head is fuzzy, my eyesight blurred. I have literally never been so aroused in my life.

'I'm sorry but I simply have to be inside you,' he admits in a low growl which despite my current physical limitations, sends every hair on the back of my neck standing on end. 'I'm physically incapable of holding off any longer.' Am I really about to know the thrill of making love to Toby Jacobs?

'Please...' I repeat. 'I'm on the pill. I just want you. Please...'

Grasping his thick cock, he swipes it gently through the channel of my slick, velvet lips, making my spine twist and tense with anticipation. I am *so* wet and swollen right now, it defies belief.

'That's an awful lot of pleading, for something you might not even enjoy,' teases Toby, knowing full well that we are going to be dynamite together.

And then, without waiting for any kind of response, he slowly starts to feed himself inside. Inhaling dramatically, I hold onto my breath as he pushes smoothly onwards. The head of his cock is bulbous and thick, immediately stretching the walls of my pussy, making me work for the pleasure I've demanded. As his entry continues, I feel each additional inch of him, sinking so incredibly deep that he touches every delicious part of me inside. It is only when his long slow entry finally ends, and I feel his groin meshing against mine, that I am capable of releasing the lungful of air I've been holding onto. Without giving me a chance to speak, Toby wraps his mouth around mine, taking full possession of me; body, heart and soul.

This amazing man sets up a rocking movement with his hips that tests every ounce of self-control I possess. Groaning into his mouth, luxuriating in the feel of his tongue sliding against my own, I grind myself against him, eager for even more. Witnessing a significant reduction in his own control, I am flooded with a cheeky surge of satisfaction. Suddenly, our mouths break apart as his hands grab for me hungrily, his thrusts much less measured.

'Go on, baby,' he growls, pumping firmly. He must have read something in my physical responses, to know that I am nearing my crescendo. It is probably the fact that my internal muscles are grasping around him, as though my life depends on it. Every outward pant I make is instantly morphing into a pained moan. 'Come hard for me,' he instructs. Just for good measure, Toby bends his head low, takes one of my rigid nipples into his mouth and chews softly.

I don't know whether it is due to his words, the seductive way he spoke them, or the effect his actions have on my overstimulated body, but clearly, I don't need to be told twice. Throwing my head backwards, a flurry of intense contractions start to milk Toby's thick cock as explosions of white light erupt across the inside of my tightly scrunched eyelids. I can just make out Toby grunting, almost as if in pain, as he tries to maintain a regular rhythm while I lose control around him. Any noise Toby makes is quickly drowned out by mine however, my screams of wondrous disbelief rebounding against the walls of his bedroom as the release is ripped from me.

No sooner do I start to descend from one climax, than Toby requires another from me. Pulling one of my legs high up to hook over his shoulder, I realise his continually thrusting cock has started to impact me much more deeply than before. A shudder passes through me as I recognise my inability to maintain any form of control. Toby is my weakness and, to be honest, I'm good with that.

'Don't stop!' I demand, sounding like a truly desperate woman, even to my own ears. 'Don't...stop...'

To his credit, Toby does exactly as I ask, driving us both on. Purposefully compressing my clit with his gently circling pelvis, it isn't long before any rhythm we might have had is long gone, our hips crashing together with increasing desperation.

'Go on!' I yelp frantically, knowing I am once again so goddamn close. Toby starts to slam into me without restraint, but his actions come at a cost.

'Oh God!' he growls, his cock now locked in a death-defying crush, thanks to his attempts to fuck his way through the force of my climaxes. 'I can't help it...' In an exciting flurry of quick, powerful thrusts followed by a roar of utter relief, Toby releases himself deep inside, pumping his juices inside me and marking me as his own. Reduced to a shuddering, gibbering, hopeless mess, it is in that single moment that I know what it is to experience pure, unadulterated bliss.

For some time, we just lay there, breathing, absorbing, recovering, as he grows softer inside my body. It feels incredibly intimate; incredibly right. Slowly, he affectionately kisses my forehead, my nose, then my quivering mouth.

'You are something else, Janie Abigail Green,' he sighs at last.

Withdrawing gently, in comparison to the furious fucking I've just been on the receiving end of, Toby bundles me up into his arms and holds on tight. I feel as though I am the most precious thing in his life; something he never wants to lose. I'm not ashamed to admit to feeling exactly the same way about him. As far as I'm concerned, after just the tiny taste of heaven I've experienced with Toby over the past few days, I'm fully signed up and officially addicted. It might have taken us a lifetime to recognise, but we have each found the missing part of ourselves, in each other.

EPILOGUE

JANIE

'Hey, Sis!' yells Mike in my direction. 'Grab us a couple more beers while you're there?'

'Yes, Sir!' I grumble, sending him a highly sarcastic, mock salute, before disappearing back into the kitchen.

I catch sight of Toby's twisted smile, caused as a result of my antics, and feel happy that I can reduce his relatively high level of stress. For not only is our episode of *Celebrity Blast from the Past* currently on the air, but we've decided to bite the bullet straight afterwards and tell Mike about our feelings for each other. We might only have formally been together for a few weeks, but we both know exactly how strongly we feel. It just feels right to be with Toby; it really is as simple as that. We exist on exactly the same wavelength, the same slightly warped humour. We have a shared history, an intense trust...oh yes, and the sex is truly on a whole different level. It is only natural that we both want to share the joy of our relationship with our nearest and dearest, which includes my brother. Unfortunately, being the one person who was always so determined that I was completely out of bounds for Toby, neither of us are relishing bringing up this exact conversation topic.

'Janie is a close family friend,' states the on-screen version of Toby.

'One of the few people who truly knows me; I hope that will always be the case.'

'But no romance?' challenges Cherry.

'She's my best friend's little sister,' shrugs the interviewed version of Toby. He doesn't enlarge further on that fact, but the way in which he spoke implied that doing anything of a romantic nature with me would be the equivalent of sacrilege. I marvel at the way Cherry accepts his blatant lie. To me, tiny micro-expressions on Toby's face give him away whenever he isn't entirely truthful, but she just drinks it all in. Of course, I do have the benefit of knowing exactly what he did to my body only a couple of hours ago. A powerful memory explodes within my mind, causing remembered shock and pleasure to turn my face crimson. Despite Toby's relatively innocent-looking appearance, he is capable of being a truly wicked man in bed.

'Awwww...' moans Mike sarcastically. 'Why does she look like she cares either way? What is it to her?'

'Search me,' sighs Toby, who I know has pretty much had enough of television producers and presenters to last him a lifetime. 'To make the programme exciting, I guess.'

'You should have told her something happened, just to give everyone a bit of hope. The audience look like they could do with perking up,' observes Mike.

Subtly, I exchange a loaded look with Toby. Is this our opportunity to confess?

'What's the presenter's name, by the way?' queries Mike, before we have a chance to tell him our precious secret. 'She's pretty hot.'

'Cherry,' groans Toby, rolling his eyes dramatically. 'Honestly, she's a nightmare.'

'You're getting far too picky in your old age,' teases Mike, taking a swig from his refreshed bottle of beer.

'Yeah, I am,' agrees Toby. He casts a glance towards me that has the capacity to strip varnish from wood and I know, unequivocally, that I will never be thought of as Plain Jane again. 'And I'm very proud of it.'

Silently, I watch the screen, as Cherry wraps up the programme and the credits start to roll.

'Mate,' murmurs Toby quietly. 'I've actually got something to tell you.'

'Oh yeah?'

'It wasn't something to be shared with the nation,' begins Toby, holding out his hand and encouraging me to sit on his knee. Immediately, Mike's jaw drops open in surprise. 'But it is something we want to share with you.'

'Seriously?' asks Mike, his eyes flashing between his sister and his best friend, silently demanding confirmation.

'I'm in love with your sister,' Toby says. His confession as good as steals the last gasp of breath from my lungs. Staring at the man of my dreams, I have no doubt that my startled expression is a mixture of disbelief, joy and adoration. For this is the first time Toby has mentioned the 'L' word. Having said that, over the past amazing weeks we've spent together almost exclusively in each other's company, we haven't attempted to hide our obvious depth of feeling for each other. As he continues to talk, it becomes clear that Toby isn't finished surprising me yet.

'The programme made a mistake. Janie isn't just my past. She's my present and, I hope, my future too,' he admits sincerely. 'I know you warned me off her several times when we were kids, but we would *really* like your blessing now.'

'I trusted you!' growls Mike accusingly. Instantly, a horrible sensation ripples through me; the two men I love most in the world, disagreeing on something so fundamental. Please don't make me choose between them. Seconds later, Mike is giggling uncontrollably, apparently highly amused by his own joke. 'Your faces!' he howls, pointing his finger between me and Toby, clutching his ribs with laughter.

'Oh, ha bloody ha,' I huff. But as I slap my brother hard on the arm for playing a trick on us, I'm aware of a huge flood of relief rushing through me.

'This is the best news ever!' grins Mike, pulling me into a tight cuddle, before hugging his best friend. 'Just wait until Mum and Dad hear about this!'

'Mum and Dad?' I ask, feeling bemused. 'Why?'

'Since we were teenagers, they've always joked to me about you two. Saying how perfect you'd be together...'

'They have?' This is the first I've heard about it.

'Yeah. Probably part of the reason I felt obliged to tell Toby to back off when we were younger. I wanted my best friend all to myself, I guess... Selfish of me. I'm sorry.'

'You're forgiven,' I grin, glancing between the two men. 'Is it okay if we share him now though?'

Dragging out the tension, Mike makes a great show of considering my proposal.

'Yeah, I think I can probably work with that,' he concedes at last.

'Hey!' complains Toby in mock offence, pulling me against his body for a huge hug. 'Don't I get any say in this?' Both Mike and I look at him with a disbelieving expression on our faces.

'Awww, bless,' grins Mike, squeezing one of Toby's cheeks between thumb and forefinger, as though speaking to a small child. 'So naive. Now, I'm going to order a celebratory Chinese takeaway!' he states, rising to his feet. 'Who's with me?'

'Yep! Definitely!' I confirm, sharing a heated glance with Toby.

'And no snogging while I'm out of the room!' chuckles Mike from the kitchen.

'Yeah, right,' I mutter. Lowering my lips to Toby's, within seconds, we are lost in each other once more. In a roundabout way, this amazing man has just declared his love for me. Nothing on God's earth could keep my hands off him right now, particularly not my big brother.

THE END

THREE DATE RULE

FENELLA ASHWORTH

CHAPTER 1

ROSE

My home telephone is ringing again. It does that a lot. Bending down to study the display, I am confronted with the words that have become increasingly familiar within recent months; Number Withheld. Immediately, an uncomfortable shiver traverses my spine and I can't help but glance towards the nearby window. I know it sounds ridiculous but I feel observed...monitored...desired. I tug the curtains firmly closed, despite the fact that dusk has only just started to encroach, and feel marginally better. On the ninth ring, the caller gives up and the sound desists.

Returning to the kitchen, I am obliged to step over the huge, grey, hairy mass of my Irish Wolfhound, Henry. Lying unhelpfully in the doorway, his whip-like tail thumps the floor, exhibiting his own form of canine amusement at the obstacle course he has set for me.

'Fuck's sake,' I mutter, as I stumble slightly, just catching myself before I fall.

Fortunately, my attention is distracted by three long beeps from the microwave signifying that dinner is ready. Henry quickly rises to his feet. Not that I'm stuck in a rut or anything, but that noise always happens just before he is fed and, consequently, he's learned to respond to it. As I place Henry's food on the floor beside his water bowl, I sigh in despair, failing to shake off an uncomfortable realisation. There is precious little difference between the appearance of his dinner and my uninspiring 'Chilli con Carne Microwave Meal for One'. Not unlike my dog, these days eating is undertaken for functional reasons, as opposed to pleasure. Unsurprisingly, we both finish our meals swiftly.

Once again, Henry knows the drill. Demonstrating he has more energy than sense, he excitedly circles beside the front door, before I've even returned my dirty cutlery to the dishwasher.

'Come on then, boy,' I sigh, unable to shake off a looming sense of dread. Pulling on my outdoor wear, I complete the ensemble by winding a long, woollen scarf around my neck. 'And *please* don't chase any deer this time,' I add, instantly recalling the trouble Henry landed me in the previous week.

I'm fortunate enough to live on a delightful country estate in the South of England, owned by one of the wealthiest families in Britain. Not only do they farm the surrounding thousand acres, but they also own a significant property portfolio, of which my rented home is just one. Troublingly, they also employ a gamekeeper whom I recently had a somewhat heated disagreement with, regarding Henry's preoccupation with the aforementioned deer.

A penetrating north wind whips across my skin, the instant I set foot outside. It is an intensely cold winter's evening and I pull on gloves without any hesitation. With my face stinging, courtesy of the elements, I encourage Henry to cross the lane and we start to trudge across the muddy field opposite my cottage. Wiping my watering eyes with the back of a gloved hand, I momentarily glance up at the ghostly outline of All Saints church, looming over the village from its exalted position upon Warren Hill. However, the church only remains visible for a matter of seconds. It is quickly engulfed by darkness, when great swirling clouds move across the sky and block out the pale moonlight again.

Thanks to Henry pulling impatiently at the leash, against my better judgement, I release him. Instantaneously he shoots forward in pursuit of countless, currently unsuspecting rabbits, leaving me quite alone. With my hands thrust deep into my pockets, I exhale audibly, before starting to climb the punishingly steep slope. I'm scarcely halfway up, when aching lungs force me to pause and catch my breath.

Squinting down the hill, it is just possible to identify our local pub, which has been the venue of many an enjoyable evening, as well as some that I'd rather forget. In glorious technicolour, one such memory pierces my mind. It was about six months ago and, against my better judgement, I'd agreed to go on a date with Bob, the local sheep farmer. Since my failed marriage, I've felt little inclination to meet new people. However, my best friend Mary applied some pressure, which I eventually caved into. The evening that followed had been an unmitigated disaster, not helped by Bob's strong agricultural odour. However, on the plus side, what I didn't know about Dorset Longhorn sheep by the end of that meal, simply wasn't worth knowing.

Continuing onwards, I acknowledge how grateful I am for having Henry in my life. I might have saved him from a cruel home the previous year, but at the same time, he has rescued me; both from my thoughts, and the innate loneliness of life. Not only does my faithful walking companion provide loyal companionship, but also an element of security. Something I'm increasingly grateful for, particularly while I continue to receive nuisance telephone calls.

Lost in my own thoughts, I'm surprised to discover that I've already reached the top of Warren Hill. It is only then that I realise this constant, loyal companionship I've been complimenting, is in extremely short supply.

'Oh no! HENRY!' I bellow across an empty landscape, no doubt sounding like the proverbial fishwife. 'HENRY! COME HERE!'

Aware of my heart beating rapidly, partly through exertion and partly through fear of having lost my dog, I purposefully take a deep, calming breath and rest against the churchyard gate. Ignoring the silence that blankets me, I whistle loudly into the chilled night air. Moonlight briefly illuminates the lichen-covered gravestones, before the swirling cloud suffocates the scene once more. I'm doing my best not to panic, but it's as spooky as fuck up here. I make a mental note to search out some alternative footpaths which don't belong in a Stephen King novel. A nearby Tawny Owl hoots, just to add to the effect, managing to freak me out slightly further. It's almost as though nature is intent on making the situation just a little bit worse. Fortunately, the eerie atmosphere is broken by the reappearance of my deeply panting hound. He promptly collapses at my feet with as much good grace as he can muster, which is actually precious little.

'Good boy!' I praise, rubbing behind Henry's fluffy ears and trying to avoid his long, whip-like tail which is being joyously thrashed about.

At that moment, I become singularly aware of our isolated solitude. An involuntary tingle encompasses the back of my skull, feeding into instinctive, primitive fears that I know better than to ignore. I feel threatened...watched. Might my mystery caller be nearby, hidden in the dark space, just beyond the boundary of the moonlight? One thing is for certain; I don't intend to hang around long enough to find out.

'Come on. Let's go,' I instruct Henry, in a voice which doesn't sound entirely like my own.

Glancing downhill, I notice some low-lying pockets of mist starting to drift inland, masking sections of our return trip. Despite this, gravity ensures our journey back down the hill is a good deal faster than the ascent. Willingly slipping into a jog, to put as much distance as possible between myself and the uncomfortable sensations I felt beside the churchyard, I suddenly lose my footing in a moonlit furrow. Experiencing that terrifying, slow-motion feeling of falling, my hands automatically fly forwards to break my descent. Having tumbled a short distance down the steep slope, I land heavily and fleetingly feel rather faint. Not always the sharpest tool in the box, Henry assumes I'm playing some kind of game and pounces on top of me, trying to lick my ears.

'Bugger off!' I groan, attempting to protect my throbbing head from the further damage my over-active canine companion seems set to inflict.

'Is there a problem?' calls out a deep voice, slicing through the darkness from a short distance away.

For all manner of reasons, I immediately fall silent. For a start, I'm never quite sure whether there is a legal right of way across this field, so there's a chance I'm currently trespassing. But more importantly, I fear this could be the man who keeps phoning me, occasionally attempting conversation. What if he's followed me here in the darkness? If he has, I'm not sure I want to know what his intentions are. I shudder slightly. It's dark here, plus I've fallen into a slight hollow in the ground. Is there a chance that I will escape notice if I continue to lie very, very still?

Of course, ordinarily my chances might have been pretty good, had I not been adjacent to a barking, wagging, wiggling Irish Wolfhound, who is marking our precise location with pinpoint accuracy. In a last-ditch effort, I attempt to rugby tackle Henry to the ground, in order to subdue him. I fail miserably.

'Are you okay?' repeats the voice, sounding more gentle and far less like a deranged stalker this time around. Through my muffled, aching brain, I'm aware of the stranger moving much closer. I glance up and see the man's great hulking mass silhouetted against the moon, which has temporarily reappeared. Henry's most ferocious-sounding bark is clearly fooling no-one.

'Erm, hello,' I venture in a quiet voice, trying to ignore my throbbing head. Through the black, impervious night, the outline of a face appears above me. His features are practically invisible in the low light, but I can just make out a square set jaw and long eyelashes. Oh, and did I mention? He smells absolutely fantastic.

CHAPTER 2

JAMES

'Hello,' I respond gently, recognising the woman's speech is slightly slurred. 'Are you hurt?'

'I'm not sure,' comes her reply. 'My head really hurts...I'm not drunk,' she adds as a clear afterthought. I'm already concerned she might have a concussion.

'Hello fella,' I smile, squatting down to provide some well-deserved attention to her dog. Swiftly, he collapses onto his back and enjoys a brief tummy tickle. I glance again towards my companion who is still sprawled on the floor. It's difficult to see her features through the darkness, but from what I *can* see, she looks incredibly pretty. I know most of the villagers but I'm fairly sure we haven't met. I would definitely have remembered. Unexpectedly, she starts to hum gently and now I'm confident she needs my help.

'Right, we must get you home. May I offer you a lift?' I notice the silhouette of her head nod gently which I take as confirmation. Carefully, I reach towards her, inhaling a sweet, floral smell that makes my senses reel.

'What are you doing?' she gasps, as I lift her easily into my arms and start to head downhill.

'Giving you a lift,' I explain, before whistling for her dog to follow us. Glancing behind briefly, I'm impressed to see he's sharp at my heels.

'I...I thought you meant in a Landrover,' she babbles, wriggling to get down. I fail to release her.

'Sorry?' I just about manage to hide the amusement in my voice.

'You don't have to *lift* me!' she struggles to explain. 'I thought you meant give me a lift in a Landrover. I'm far too heavy!'

'Nonsense.' There's hardly anything to her. 'Just relax. We'll have you back home shortly.'

For an instant, a break in the clouds allows the pale moonlight to illuminate her features. I was right in my previous assumption; she's beautiful, and my chest reacts accordingly. Unfortunately, just then, her eyes close and we miss the opportunity to share a glance. Trustingly, she rests her head against my soft woollen jumper. Seconds later, the moonlight disappears and I can admire her no more.

'Mmmm. Christmas...saddle soap...sweet yet masculine,' she mumbles.

'Say again?' I reply with a chuckle, this time completely failing to hide my amusement.

'You smell amazing,' she sighs contentedly.

'You think so, huh?'

'Yeah. You obviously don't farm Dorset Longhorns. If you did, you wouldn't smell like rocky road made with extra marshmallows,' she adds confidentially. 'Combined with sticky toffee apples and a comforting mug of frothy hot chocolate on a cold day.'

'Wow! Thank you. And would there be whipped cream on the hot chocolate too?'

'Mmmmm, definitely,' she groans with pleasure. 'And chocolate sprinkles over the top.'

'Sounds like a diabetics worst nightmare,' I observe dryly.

'Or a chocoholics wet dream,' she quickly counters.

Before I have a chance to respond to such a surprising comment, she starts to hum again. This time, it sounds suspiciously like the tune to "I'm Henry the Eighth, I am, I am".

Holding her body slightly closer to mine, I approach the lane feeling an incredible sense of connection to this woman which I simply can't explain. I wait until she reaches the end of the chorus before I interrupt her.

'We're back on the road. Tell me where you live.'

'Honeysuckle cottage. It's just...'

'Yeah, I know where it is,' I smile, heading in the right direction and arriving much sooner than I would have liked. I could literally hold her all night.

'I must repay you for your kindness!' she exclaims, as we reach her home and I nudge the garden gate open with my knee. 'Let me cook you dinner tomorrow evening!'

'Oh, that sounds lovely, thank you.' Anything to spend more time with this woman, whose name I haven't even been able to ascertain yet. 'Well, you're back home,' I announce, just in case she isn't aware. Curiously though, I fail to lower her to the ground, instead just remaining as we are, with her cradled gently in my arms.

'My hero,' she sighs contentedly, before dropping an unexpected kiss on my cheek. I act instinctively, turning my head to meet hers, until our mouths are aligned. Gazing intently into each other's eyes, I notice a flicker of doubt pass across her face, before being replaced by a low groan of surrender. As I lower my head and allow our lips to graze each other for the first time, I know full well that I'm taking advantage. But she smells so sweet, her lips so plump and infinitely kissable, that I just can't help myself. Straightaway, a needy growl escapes from low down in her throat which sets my senses alight.

Gathering her more firmly into my arms, I intensify our kiss, eventually allowing my tongue to teasingly explore. She responds in kind and as her fingers slide into my hair, pulling me deeper, our coupling quickly moves from being relatively chaste, towards something wickedly wanton. Part of my brain is aware that she is likely concussed, so my behaviour is every kind of wrong, but I'm way past caring. Groaning in despair, I am entirely trapped under her spell.

'I'm sorry,' I mutter, eventually finding the strength to pull away. Carefully, I lower her down to the porch, to stand on her own two feet. Aware of my cock throbbing unbearably, I adjust my jacket to sit more firmly around my hips, in an attempt to hide my obvious arousal.

'Er...would you like to come in?' she stutters, clearly attempting to be polite, despite her confused state.

'I think it's safer if I stay outside, don't you?' I murmur, undoubtedly causing her to flush slightly. I can only imagine the scenario we might end up in, if I'm permitted entry into her home tonight... 'But I am going to insist on waiting here, until you phone someone to be with you. I'm a bit concerned you might have a concussion. Unless you normally sing to strangers and offer them such effusive compliments, that is?' I add, unable to prevent my lips from twitching into a smile.

'No, I don't usually,' she confides, trawling through her coat pockets for the key and managing to unlock her front door. 'This is definitely a one off.'

Grappling in the darkness for the light switch, she flicks it on, simultaneously turning to look back at me. I can't help but inhale swiftly, astonished by the clarity of her brilliant blue eyes. Temporarily, I am completely lost for words and simply gaze at her in astonishment. The only positive aspect to the situation is that she looks similarly floored.

'Err...err...' she stutters in disbelief. There is little doubt she has recognised the identity of her rescuer.

'James Stirling,' I mutter. It seems slightly superfluous to offer my hand in greeting, given that we've just snogged the life out of each other moments before, but I do it all the same.

'Rose,' she whispers in response. The feel of her gloved hand squeezing mine sends my body into disarray once again. 'Rose Jackson.'

'Go and call a friend, Rose,' I request gently. 'I'll wait here while you do.'

She nods, releases my hand and walks into her home, trustingly leaving the front door slightly ajar. I hear a muttered conversation and less than a minute later, she has returned.

'I've phoned my friend, Mary. She's on her way round now.'

'Good,' I praise. Flicking through the contents of my pockets, I pull out a business card. 'Just in case you need any further help, here are my contact details,' I state, passing the card across to Rose. It's a feeble attempt at giving her my number, but there it is. I want her to have the ability to contact me and now she does.

'Thank you.'

'What time would you like me to arrive tomorrow evening...if your earlier offer of dinner still stands?' I add, watching her face fall in slow motion. Perhaps, now she knows who I am, she has no interest in seeing me again? The realisation hits me unexpectedly hard. I have an urge to get to know this woman so much better. And I would do pretty much anything to experience another one of those decadent kisses.

'Seven?' she gulps.

'Seven it is,' I smile, aware of someone approaching fast up the road. I automatically assume it's her friend and start to back away. 'Goodnight then, Rose.'

'Goodnight, James,' she replies mechanically, still gripping tightly onto the door frame.

'Good evening,' I say politely to a wild-eyed, wild-haired woman who scurries past me with her mouth hanging open. I can only assume this is Mary.

'Yeah...' is all she replies with. Pulling up my collar to protect me from the worst of the cruel wind, I stride purposefully into the night, but not before I hear Mary's muttered words floating on the wind.

'Holy fuck! Do you know who that was?'

CHAPTER 3

ROSE

Having watched him walk down the lane and into the night, I close the door gently, knowing that my lightheaded feeling has little to do with the knock I sustained to my head.

'Tell me! Tell me!' demands Mary, as I stumble into the lounge, leaning heavily on the back of the sofa.

'I hit my head out on a walk. James found me and brought me home,' I explain simply, suddenly feeling pretty rough. 'Do you mind just keeping an eye on me while I lie down. I really don't feel that great.'

'Sure,' murmurs Mary, quickly leaping into the mode she's so used to inhabiting during her daytime role as a nurse.

I don't know how long I sleep for, but it must have been a good few hours. When I wake briefly, I discover Mary snoring on the double bed beside me. Rolling my blurry eyes towards the bedside table, I squint at the clock, eventually concluding that it's still the middle of the night. With a grunt of relief, I rapidly drift back into unconsciousness once more. My body undoubtedly requires more sleep. I'll leave worrying about the whole James situation until tomorrow. Hopefully then, I'll be refreshed enough to think about it, without feeling my toes curl in embarrassment.

When I wake again the following morning, it is to the sound of rain pounding on the windowpanes and the smell of cooking bacon emanating from the kitchen. Recognising I feel a damn sight better than the previous night, I grab my dressing gown and slippers and head off to find Mary.

'Morning!' she calls with a grin, flipping bacon in a carefree way. Predictably, Henry is drooling at her feet, shadowing her every move.

'Hi,' I sigh, slumping down at the kitchen table and helping myself to a well-deserved coffee from the cafetière. For a short time there is silence, while Mary dishes up two bacon sandwiches.

'So, are you going to make me beg?' she demands at last, in a manner of someone bursting with meddlesome interest. 'James Stirling,' she clarifies, when all I do is raise my eyebrows questioningly.

'Oh God!' I groan, immediately hunching over my steaming drink, hoping the soothing vapours might resolve the situation for me. They don't. 'I invited him for dinner tonight.'

'What?' my friend yelps, fully aware that I can't cook for the life of me.

'He accepted... What am I going to do?'

'Well, you've got a number of options,' Mary replies, causing me to experience a sudden surge of optimism. Options are good.

'Firstly, you could call him and cancel...apologise and explain you've made a terrible mistake?' smirks Mary, intuitively appreciating I would hate that idea. Just the horrified look on my face confirms her suspicions.

'Or secondly,' she continues, clearly on a roll. 'You can stop moping around and get ready to have a lovely evening.'

A pause follows and I screw up my face slightly.

'Any other options?' Those two seem a bit limiting.

'I guess there's always emigration, sudden death, or how about being diagnosed with a very contagious disease?' replies Mary. For a brief time, my interest lingers on the final option, but then reality kicks in. My best friend is being sarcastic. Perhaps I am still a little concussed, if it takes me that long to realise.

'Oh, come on!' complains Mary. 'He's a very rich, very handsome guy. I honestly don't see the problem.'

'The problem?' I repeat incredulously. 'I'll tell you the problem! James Stirling is the son of one of the wealthiest men in England. He's been educated at Eton and Cambridge and goodness knows where else. He's a rich, classy, handsome, very eligible guy and I'm so completely way out of his league, it's laughable.'

'Don't say th ...'

'Furthermore,' I continue forcefully, blocking what would undoubtedly be Mary's encouraging support. 'As his family own half the properties in the village, including this one, I've got a feeling he is, albeit indirectly, probably also my landlord.'

'Well, you must have made enough of an impression last night, for him to want to spend the evening with you,' Mary attempts to rally. As she's talking, I'm reminded of the way he carried me home. He'd barely been puffing, despite his additional, and not insubstantial load.

'I beg to differ,' I reply dryly. 'I hummed *I'm Henry the Eighth* to him and told him he smelt like a chocoholic's wet dream.' Something stops me from admitting that we also exchanged an incredibly steamy kiss, in full view of the village, although in my defence, it was dark. Mary's jaw dropped visibly.

'Why?' she asks in obvious astonishment.

'I was concussed,' I reply crossly. 'I don't want to think about it.'

'Well, this situation is entirely salvageable.'

'How?' I ask in a tone that clearly doesn't agree with her statement.

'By me coming round after work to cook dinner for you. Then all you need to do is follow some very simple instructions, look gorgeous and enjoy yourself.'

'You really think we can get away with that?'

'I know we can,' she grins, just as the shrill ring of my home phone interrupts our conversation. Ignoring it, I grab my friend's hand across the table and squeeze tightly.

'I don't deserve you!'

'Nobody does!' she laughs. 'That's why I'm single. Are you going to answer that? Might be your super-hot date!'

'Um...okay,' I sigh. Leaning across, I grab the phone with a sense of foreboding and hold it to my ear. 'Hello?' Silence.

'What do you want?' I demand, sounding more than a little shaky. Mary glances across at me enquiringly, but I ignore her.

'I want to talk with you,' admitted a man's voice that sends shivers down my spine. It is very rare that he dares to speak and I find it a worrying development that his confidence is undoubtedly growing.

'Who are you? For God's sake, leave me alone!'

'I can see you've got company,' explains the voice, immediately doubling my crippling fear. My eyes dart towards the front window. Was he outside the house? He'd never gone that far before.

'I'll phone back later.' Then the line went dead.

'Was that him again?' Mary demands, her glance full of concern.

I nod and sigh.

'You've *got* to report this. This has gone way too far,' my friend states forcefully.

'I know. But I don't even know who he is.'

'But the police could...'

'Besides,' I interrupt. 'I have Henry for protection.'

'Protection?!' she baulks. Okay, so I might have just over-exaggerated my canine's skillset.

'Mary,' I state in the most forceful tone I can muster. 'I'm not going to let this weirdo control my life!'

'Fine,' she huffs, gathering up her belongings and heading for the door. 'I'll be over this afternoon to help you prepare for your hot date.'

'Thank you,' I reply meekly, suddenly feeling guilty for raising my voice at my good friend, who has nothing but my very best interests at heart.

'Oooh! And make sure you Google him!'

'Google him?' I repeat in astonishment.

'Mmm-hmm. Definitely,' she confirms with a wicked grin, before closing the door behind herself.

LATER THAT EVENING, my cottage is unusually clean and tidy. The overall atmosphere of domesticity is further enhanced by the delicious smell of Mary's beef stroganoff emanating temptingly from the kitchen. All that I require now is a dinner guest to share it with. Even Henry has been groomed, much to his disgust, and is now snoring peacefully beside the crackling fire. His feet twitch occasionally, during particularly exciting rabbit chasing sequences taking place in his dreams.

Going against Mary's advice, I haven't taken to the internet to find out more about James. I'd much rather find out about him in person, than via some wildly inaccurate, largely spurious source. I don't have long to wait. At just a couple of minutes after our agreed meeting time, the doorbell rings and the swarm of butterflies currently taking up residence in my tummy, shift into overdrive. Predictably, Henry makes his noisy way to the front of the house, to welcome our guest.

Swinging the door open, my breath fleetingly catches in my throat. Finding such a stunning man standing on my front porch, I feel quite overwhelmed. At that moment, I want nothing more than to soak up everything I can about the delectable James. He's probably a few years older than me, in his late thirties I estimate. Hungrily, I take in every detail, from his damp, recently-washed, jet-black hair through to his sparkling blue eyes, toned body and obvious height. God, he's divine! To think we've already shared an extremely steamy snog, which is all but guaranteed to be repeated tonight, sends a throb of anticipation through my abdomen. And it is only in that very instant that a horrible question flits through my mind. James couldn't be my telephone stalker...could he?

CHAPTER 4

JAMES

My first glimpse of Rose, illuminated by the low, evening sun sends a bolt of desire straight through me. It also acts as a powerful reminder, in no uncertain terms, as to exactly why I kissed her so passionately the previous night. She is glorious. Wearing a short, red dress, it seems to accentuate her every curve, while displaying her dainty legs to perfection. But before we even manage to share a greeting, a change in her facial expression takes place before my very eyes; apprehension, and perhaps a little fear, is now her over-riding countenance.

'Good evening,' I say cautiously in greeting.

'Hi,' she replies, any familiarity we'd built up previously, now entirely absent.

'Everything okay?'

'Er...sure,' she confirms, failing to meet my eyes. 'Please do come in.'

'Thanks.' Ducking my head slightly, I step into the cottage. 'How are you feeling?'

'Oh...yes...much better, thanks to you,' she replies, still somewhat distracted. Henry, on the other hand, has no such qualms, bounding up to me as though I'm a long-lost friend. Briefly I squat down to say hello.

'I've just brought a little something for you,' I announce, once Henry's focus has been directed elsewhere. Calmly, I present Rose with an enormous bouquet of flowers which I'd been holding behind my back. Rose looks quite overwhelmed when she takes them, as though she is rarely in receipt of gifts. Her reaction makes her seem unexpectedly vulnerable. 'And these,' I add, pulling two bottles of wine from the deep pockets of my Barbour jacket, before shrugging the garment off and hanging it up on a hook by the door.

'You really didn't have to...' she stutters. 'I'm supposed to be thanking you, not the other way around.'

'As a rule, I don't tend to subscribe to standard etiquette,' I shrug.

'I'll open up a bottle of wine,' she announces nervously, scuttling through to the kitchen. I follow behind at a much more leisurely pace, admiring how beautifully she keeps her home and appreciating the incredible smell emanating from the oven.

Shortly afterwards, we are back in the lounge, seated in front of a roaring log fire and making somewhat stilted conversation, when the phone starts to ring. Instantly, Rose's demeanour changes; sitting bolt upright, her body visibly stiffens as she glances towards the front curtains which are tightly drawn. I'm not sure if she's confused, frightened, troubled, or all three, but something is definitely going on.

'Are you going to answer that?' I enquire gently, after it has rung five times and she's made no movement towards the phone.

'No,' she replies, shaking her head gently, sending her long, blonde locks into disarray. She is desperately trying to hide it, but the worry on her face is evident. And all the while, the telephone continues to ring.

'Do you mind if I do then?' I ask gently. She shrugs almost imperceptibly, but I take it as my authorisation to act. Striding across the room, I pick up the receiver and, without speaking, listen carefully. Meanwhile, Rose concentrates unnaturally hard on Henry, who is snoring peacefully on the fireside rug. For a while, all I can hear is deep breathing. Then, at last, a voice.

'I'm back, Rose. Just like I promised earlier...'

'Who is this?' I demand in a voice of unnatural calm. I'm aware of an ache in my left hand, which has subconsciously balled into a tight fist. Meanwhile, an angry pulse throbs in my head and the quilt of muscles in my jaw receive an unexpected workout. What the fuck is going on here? An ex-boyfriend? A stalker? Whoever he is, just one look at Rose's demeanour tells me that his attentions are entirely unsolicited. He's certainly a coward because the instant he hears my voice, he hangs up. Carefully, I replace the handset as Rose visibly relaxes before my very eyes. And then suddenly, it all becomes clear.

'You thought I could be him, didn't you?'

'Er...um...for a moment, possibly...' she stumbles.

'I'm not,' I confirm, studying her carefully. 'And I would never do anything like that.'

'I know.'

'Good. How long has this been going on for?'

'Dunno exactly. Four months?' she guesses.

'Jesus,' I groan. 'And you haven't reported him?'

Looking guilt-ridden, she shakes her head in reply.

'Have you got any idea who he is?'

'None at all...' That's disappointing because, as far as I'm concerned, he definitely sounded familiar. I'm unable to pinpoint exactly who the guy is, but I'm convinced he's local. I decide not to share my theory with Rose though; we don't need her any more freaked out than she obviously already is.

'Can I interest you in a hug?' I query. She looks so forlorn that it's the only thing I can think of, to help cheer her up. With a shy smile, she nods, dropping her eyes to her lap. I sit close beside her on the sofa and hold out an arm, silently encouraging her to shuffle her body towards me. With an uncertain glance in my direction, she lays a hand tentatively on my abdomen and places her ear against my chest. Immediately, I inhale sharply. God, it feels so good to simply hold, and be held.

With one arm wrapped around her shoulder, my spare hand gently caresses her soft hair. In next to no time, Rose is breathing in synchronisation with my stroking hand, sounding incredibly content.

'Is this dangerous?' I ask with a small smile. My semi-erect cock is already providing me with an answer to that question, but I'm interested to hear what Rose has to say, all the same.

'Why?' she groans. My hand has started to migrate temptingly towards the nape of her neck, eliciting deep breaths which are occasionally interspersed with light, submissive whimpers.

'After last night...or have you forgotten about that already?' I grin, the memory of our kiss as clear to me, as if it had happened seconds earlier.

'Of course not,' she sighs. 'How could I...'

'It's just, when we're so close, I can easily do this...' I murmur, before placing a kiss on the top of her head. In surprise, Rose straightens up slightly and turns to face me. Our mouths are inches apart now, my focus instinctively darting between her eyes and her lips, trying to second guess her response.

'Or this...' she replies at last, soft fingers reaching up to brush temptingly across my top lip. A low growl I hadn't anticipated, escapes in an uncontrolled manner from deep within my throat. Given that, seconds later, she still hasn't removed her fingers from my reach, I find myself unable to prevent what comes entirely naturally; my soft tongue slips out of my mouth, encircles one of her fingertips, and encourages it to slide between my lips.

In my confusion, I'm not sure if the low groan which issues forth into the room, originates from Rose, myself or a combination of both of us, but I recognise it as a green light to continue, nevertheless. Tenderly, I kiss her forehead, each of her fluttering eyelids and the very tip of her nose, before working my way towards her soft, plump lips. Unfortunately, just as my mouth brushes against hers, causing her to emit a gasp that I know I could easily become addicted to the sound of, a loud, wailing alarm fills the house.

'Oh shit!' she yelps, her body stiffening beside me.

'What's happening?' I mutter, my throbbing cock making me feel far less worried about whether the house is on fire, than I should be.

In horror, we both watch as a plume of black smoke rises, ghost-like towards us.

'Fuck!' I yelp. Rushing into the kitchen, I quickly ascertain the damage. Having turned off the oven and removed the charred remains of a once-edible meal from within its depths, I fling open the windows and doors, allowing the cold night air to rush in.

'Bugger!' Rose mutters, disconnecting the batteries from the multiple smoke alarms, to help silence Henry's howling. 'I forgot about dinner. Please tell me you aren't my landlord! Given you've witnessed me almost burn down my home, my security deposit would be screwed.'

'I'm not your landlord.' The white lie falls easily from my mouth. It's clear she'd be appalled to find out I am, plus I have no desire to alter the dynamic of our fledgling relationship in that way. One day, I'll own to it, but not tonight.

Glancing around the small room in amusement, I observe a slightly charred note from her friend Mary, providing clear culinary instructions, along with a sign hanging jauntily on the wall. It reads:

"Many people have eaten here and gone on to lead near-normal lives."

It's at that moment that our eyes lock and we both start to laugh. Having started, it's clear that neither of us can stop. Before long, I am forced to wipe away the tears coursing down my cheeks. With one hand clutching my aching side, it takes a while before we are capable of speech once more. It's a cathartic experience which suddenly makes me appreciate that I haven't felt such uninhibited, spontaneous joy since childhood.

'Okay, full disclosure,' says Rose, at last. 'I can't cook for the life of me. I'm a disaster in the kitchen.'

She might be a disaster in the kitchen, but I'm quite willing to bet she's a fucking delight in bed. I observe her carefully, acknowledging that we're at a crossroads. If we return to the sofa, I'd willingly bet that the only thing we'll be consuming tonight is each other. But something inside me wants to allow ourselves to be better acquainted first.

'Go and get your coat on,' I mutter, hoping I'm making the right call. 'I'm taking you to the pub for dinner.'

'You are?' She sounds surprised, as though the failure of her culinary abilities might somehow make me less interested in her, when in fact the opposite is true.

'Yeah. It's either that, or take you to bed,' I admit, not oblivious to the excited look in her eyes. 'And I can't do that because it would break my three date rule.'

'Your three date rule?' she giggles. 'I thought you didn't subscribe to standard etiquette?'

'Well on this occasion, possibly against my better judgement, I do.'

CHAPTER 5

JAMES

My eyes dart across the room to observe Rose seated at a corner table in our village pub, beside the gently flickering log fire. She looks nervous, probably not helped by the occasional covert glance she's receiving from the locals, no doubt trying to work out what our connection is. This village thrives on gossip; perhaps it was a mistake for me to suggest eating here, but I wanted to go somewhere I knew Rose would feel safe. Particularly given what's been happening in her personal life, of late.

Having placed our food order at the bar, I collect two glasses and a bottle of white wine, before returning to our table. I observe Rose purposefully placing her mildly trembling palms flat on her lap as I approach. I'm glad I'm not the only one feeling apprehensive here.

'Don't look so worried,' I smile reassuringly, sending her a brief wink. Almost immediately, the red flush on her neck and face deepens and she chews slightly on her lower lip. God, the woman is adorable; her reactions are so comfortingly honest. Every synapse in my brain is screaming at me to take her to bed right now but, for some reason, I'm intent on behaving properly.

'S...sorry,' she stutters, her voice sounding high and strained.

'You're quite safe here with me,' I explain soothingly.

'I am?' Is it my imagination, or does she sound slightly disappointed by that statement.

'Well...yeah, kind of,' I grin, lowering my voice dramatically, lest we are overheard. 'Being in public will force me to keep my hands to myself.'

Our eyes briefly lock and, save for the crackling log fire, a silence extends between us. Without a shadow of a doubt, we are revelling in our mutual desire to hold each other close once more and enjoy the astonishingly sensual kisses I know we are capable of.

'I guess I should be grateful we're in public then,' she chuckles, glancing around the room. Being midweek and the middle of winter, very few people are patronizing the establishment; in addition to Jim, the landlord, there are just a couple of the die-hard regulars, perched on bar stools, pint in hand.

'You certainly should be,' I confirm.

Once our initial nerves pass, we quickly relax and begin to thoroughly enjoy each other's company. Progressing efficiently through our first bottle of wine and the main course, our conversation is easy-going, gossipy and unexpectedly amusing. Occasionally, our feet brush purposefully against each other, or our fingers briefly intertwine, before remembering where we are. Increasingly, it is becoming obvious that we neither want to, or are capable of keeping our hands off each other.

After our dessert order has been given to a hovering Jim, there is a temporary break in conversation, during which my eyes scan the room. I can't help but notice we are being very closely watched by Ben Fowler. Working in the library of the nearby town, he's a villager who has always struck me as a slightly odd man. The intensity with which he's observing Rose disturbs me and it's in that instant, I know.

'Ben?' I say, raising my voice to ensure it carries across the room. I'm aware of having to funnel all of my concentration into suppressing the anger which I can already sense is bubbling away beneath the surface. 'Why don't you come and sit with us?'

Rose looks slightly surprised that I would invite a third party into our increasingly intimate meal, but to her credit, she takes it in her stride. Looking decidedly uncomfortable, Ben skulks across the room and hovers awkwardly beside us.

'Sit down,' I instruct, in a manner not to be argued with. Ben does as I order and I try to ignore a flash of surprise that passes across Rose's face, in response to the terse way I've just spoken to him. I hope she'll understand both my brusque attitude, and my apparent rudeness at not formally introducing the two of them. Something tells me that she won't thank me for actively encouraging her to unwittingly shake the hand of a man who has made her life a misery for months.

'H...hello, Sir,' stutters Ben. Failing to make eye contact with us, he looks somewhat nauseous.

'We've already spoken today, haven't we Ben?' I ask. Briefly he looks confused, until the truth eventually dawns on him.

'I...I...'

'You remember?' I query, able to feel the pulse in my temple beating with anger. 'On the phone, at Rose's house?'

Instantly, I hear Rose gasp and recoil slightly beside me. Quietly, I cover one of her hands with my own, to provide silent reassurance and strength.

'You?!' she exclaims, observing Ben with shock.

'You've met before?' I query, genuinely interested.

'I was in here having a drink with Mary, earlier this year,' Rose started to explain, apparently unable to stop staring at Ben. 'He came over and offered to buy us drinks. Wouldn't take no for an answer... Why would you do something so cruel?' she asks, shaking her head. I find myself praying that I'm never on the receiving end of the disgusted expression that's currently on her face.

'Are you going to answer the lady?' I demand, but I can tell that the answer is no. After all, how can you defend the indefensible. In all honesty, I'm not sure Rose needs an answer, when what happened seems pretty clear to me. Unlike most normal people who would simply shrug off the girls' refusal to engage and move on, Ben perceived himself to be rejected, insulted even. Feeling wounded, he set about seeking vindication. However, I do find it interesting that his focus was centred on Rose and not Mary, or even both of them. That element, I don't have an answer for.

'So, what happens now?' breathes Rose, when no response is forthcoming.

'It's really up to you,' I explain gently. 'Of course, you are well within your rights to press charges. Stalking is a criminal offence...'

'Stalking?' questions Ben stupidly, looking seriously afraid. 'Surely, I...'

'Stalking,' I confirm, interrupting what would doubtless be his pathetic explanations. Part of me would like to see Ben prosecuted for what he's done, although I also appreciate that there is extremely little evidence. Unfortunately, there's always the chance that Rose could go through what would undoubtedly be a stressful and difficult process, only to find Ben cleared of all charges. I'd like to provide an alternative solution for consideration.

'The decision is entirely yours,' I explain to Rose, gently squeezing the hand I still hold in mine. 'There is no immediate time limit for you to report this to the police. So how about we simply say to Ben that his behaviour stops right now. Without question. He never attempts to contact you again, either by phone or any other method. If he sees you in the street, he simply walks the other way. Not only will you go straight to the police, if he fails to abide by this request, but I will ensure his wife is made fully aware of his extra-curricular interests and he is suspended as a school governor, pending an enquiry.' There have to be some benefits to my position in society, and possessing a very strong influence over the local community is one of them.

Rose's eyes open a little wider and stare at me for confirmation. Apparently, she didn't know he was married. To be fair, it was an easy mistake to make. Ben had also clearly forgotten about the existence of the poor, long-suffering Mrs Fowler too.

'This is your only warning, Ben,' I state in a cold, hard voice, turning my head to face him full on. 'After tonight, I suggest you keep an *extremely* low profile. Shall we?' I add gently to Rose.

With a small nod, she willingly accepts my proffered arm, looping her hand through it and holding on tight. As we walk towards the exit,

I cancel our dessert order and drop some cash on the bar. I can't imagine she wants to stay here any longer than I do now.

Having exited the pub, we start to take the short stroll through our village, back towards her home. It's much colder now, the moon and stars shining brightly down upon us from the great expanse of space.

'You were completely awesome!' states Rose, apparently unable to hide both her relief at being free from her stalker and her admiration at my involvement. Immediately, I feel a powerful blast of heat spreading through my chest, which makes me feel a little lightheaded.

'As were you,' I admit. I reposition my arm around her shoulders, hugging tightly. It feels so damn right, that I simply leave it there. 'Tell me, do you have eggs, milk and flour back at your house?'

Rose turns to look at me in astonishment and I can't help but laugh out loud. I find it amusing that I continue to surprise her. People often assume that because I've been brought up within an upper class family, that I'll act in a certain way. It's always a thrill to prove them wrong.

'I do...' she replies cautiously.

'Excellent. You missed out on your dessert at the pub tonight, so I'm planning to cook you crêpes.'

'You're obviously a much better chef than I am,' she giggles, gazing up at me in a way that makes my cock twitch with longing. 'I should have just got you to cook us dinner tonight, rather than Mary.'

'How about I cook you dinner tomorrow, then?' I murmur intimately.

'Tomorrow?' she says, shyly.

'Tomorrow,' I confirm, wondering if I have the willpower to walk away from her tonight.

CHAPTER 6

ROSE

Oh God. My throat is dry, my limbs are trembling, my head is fuzzy. I honestly can't think straight. It's like when you know something monumental is just about to happen and the looming anticipation simply becomes too much. Like reaching the summit of a huge rollercoaster and hovering, abandoned at the top; the subsequent thrill is inevitable and yet maybe it isn't. Maybe what you're expecting to happen, might not take place at all?

As promised, James has cooked the most exquisite crêpes, to which we have added copious amounts of sweet toppings. Still finishing the final mouthfuls, we are intimately curled up on my sofa watching a comedy on the television. Except, of course, my concentration is perhaps five percent on the programme and ninety-five percent on James. It would be less than five percent, but I need to ensure I laugh at the appropriate times, to prevent myself looking like a wide-eyed, sexually inexperienced fool.

Nevertheless, I'm aware of each and every touch point of our bodies. Our knees, our elbows, occasionally our feet and fingers. As it is, I'm almost bubbling over with desire. Thanks to my previous concussion, I know the kiss we shared last night was phenomenal, but it is a little hazy in my memory. I'd definitely like to rectify that.

'Have you finished?' murmurs James, nodding towards the empty plate I'm now holding in my hands. I hadn't been aware he was watching me, thanks to my wandering mind.

'Yes,' I croak, feeling strangely exposed, now the activity of eating has been removed from the equation and I can evade our intimacy no longer.

'I beg to differ,' he smirks, sending me a long, hard stare that has the capacity to turn my insides to liquid. 'You've left some chocolate sauce on your plate.'

I glance down with a frown. Hardly. Short of licking it up, I'm not sure how he expects me to consume it. Intent on proving me wrong, James unexpectedly lifts my right hand, isolating my index finger. Then, with a boyish grin, he swipes my fingertip through the chocolate, holding it between us, as the sauce slowly slides down my finger under gravity.

'Wha...?' I start to ask, before it becomes blatantly obvious what he's planning. Leaning towards me, he takes the tip of my finger between his lips, sucking gently. The dual combination of his soft, moist mouth on my skin, coupled with the intensity of desire in his eyes, sends a shudder of lust straight through me. Flashing me a brief wink that somehow makes my entire body clench down hard, his tongue slides down my finger to capture the escaping sauce, sending my thoughts into further disarray.

Fuck. I can feel every flick of his highly capable tongue. There can't be any chocolate sauce left now, but still he continues, eyes closed in apparent pleasure. My clit is pulsing hard as my subconscious mind considers what that talented mouth of his would feel like, on other more sensitive regions.

Unable to prevent myself, the rest of my hand curves around his chiselled, prickly jaw, stroking tenderly. With my spare hand, I reach for him, encouraging one of his fingers into my own mouth, where I imagine it is a much more exciting part of his anatomy. He tastes as good as he smells and I am overwhelmed with a need to devour him. With each playful suck or flick, I can feel his moan vibrating down the length of my finger, as he continues to tease.

Quickly, it becomes too much. We both sense an urgent need to be closer. I'm grateful when James makes his move, because if he hadn't, I was just about to. With an animal-like groan, he releases my finger from his mouth and scrambles across to my side of the sofa, efficiently trapping me beneath him. Gazing up in disbelief, my entire body throbs with an intense need, as I willingly surrender to his demands. I feel primed. Carnal. Wanton. As far as I'm concerned, right now, I'm signed up to whatever he's offering.

'You are so beautiful,' he sighs, sending a fluttering thrill through my chest.

Slowly, his mouth lowers towards mine. In a reflex reaction, my eyes roll closed as my lips open up to accept him. The first touch is tender, teasing, playful; everything I imagine this incredible man will be like in bed. As I reciprocate, our kiss deepens, the sensations that our mouths prove capable of creating, verging on being overwhelming. He slightly readjusts his position and I'm instantly aware of his thick length pressed against my thigh, swiftly making me feel even wetter than I already am. I'm not sure I've ever desired another human being more.

The first time I feel his tongue take charge of mine, I become so lightheaded that I don't doubt I'd have fallen over, had I not already been horizontal. I groan deep down in my throat, wordlessly begging for more, encouraging him to continue. Feeling beyond turned on, my fingers are exploring boldly now; his hair, neck, shoulders, back, tight ass, muscled thighs. Every new delicacy that I discover feels better than the last. Curling my fingers around the base of his shirt, I manage to untuck it from his trousers and slide my hand inside, stroking his soft, warm skin. Divine. That's the only word I've got to describe him.

'I *really* ought to go!' James exclaims, practically leaping up from the sofa in a manner that suggests he is having to forcefully withdraw, very much against his will. Striding towards the front door, he shrugs on his coat, but not before I've got an eyeful of the swollen protrusion in his trousers. A battle is undoubtedly currently taking place between his mind and his body and, call me cruel, but I find that as sexy as fuck. It's a scenario I wish to test out a little further.

'Do you have to?' I ask playfully, unfurling myself from the sofa and padding towards him.

'You know I do,' he complains, fastening up his Barbour jacket. Immediately, my fingers reach for his zip and pull it back down again. Courageously, I slide my hand inside his coat, stroking the outline of his abs, down to his hip, where I circle the area slowly.

'Fuck me...' he grunts in a low, rumbling voice, his eyes temporarily rolling closed as he leans against the wall.

Without looking, his hand reaches out for me, making contact. As we jointly sigh, he strokes the curve of my waist before heading up my ribcage. I start to gasp as he shows no sign of stopping, sliding along the underside of my breast. Expertly, his thumb finds my nipple through my clothing and playfully teases. I all but collapse against him. I can feel arousal flowing freely into my panties by this point; I need this man more than life itself.

'Two can play at that game,' he manages to mutter over my breathy moans.

Determined not to be beaten, I run the backs of my fingers towards his groin, until I locate the thick, swollen length of him. Within moments, his eyes have snapped back open, looking lustful and determined. Encompassing my wrists in his strong grip, James spins me around, trapping me between himself and the wall, holding my hands high above my head in an unexpected position of surrender.

'Jesus Christ,' he manages to mutter, accompanied with a shuddering inhale. 'What the fuck are you trying to do to me?'

'Turn you on?' I suggest, gazing up at him with an impish smile.

'Mission accomplished,' he admits, swallowing with obvious effort. Incredibly, his upper class English accent sounds even sexier, when high levels of arousal force him to grunt out his responses.

As though in slow motion, giving the impression he can't help himself, James gently lowers his lips to mine. Pinned down by his body and held firm, I can do no more than accept and reciprocate, not that there is anything else I'd rather be doing. And there, he kisses me goodnight; very properly, very sensually, very thoroughly. When, at last, he pulls away, my lips feel bruised from the power of his kiss, the skin around my mouth sensitive from the pressure of his stubble digging into my face. It's the sweetest pain I've ever known.

'I'll see you tomorrow?' he murmurs, as he releases my wrists and opens the front door. I can't help but wonder if any nosy neighbours will see us and question what the well-respected, much admired, currently slightly dishevelled James Stirling is doing, spending time with the likes of me. If they knew the truth, which is that I basically fell over in a field and then almost set fire to my own home, I have a feeling they'd be far from impressed. God, I can be such a muppet sometimes! And yet, despite my apparent ineptitude, tonight couldn't have turned out much better.

'Come over to mine tomorrow?' he continues, glancing back at me with a look of regret seeping through his handsome features. I get the impression he'd quite happily ignore his dating rule on this occasion, but propriety has won…this time, at least. 'About half six? For dinner…and other stuff,' he smirks. Purposefully, he thrusts his hands in his pockets and walks away, which is just as well. I have a feeling that we are both teetering on the edge of control. One more touch and I'd have dragged him into my bedroom, the three date rule be damned. Fuck. How am I ever going to make it through the next few hours, until we next meet?

CHAPTER 7

JAMES

As I glance at the clock for the hundredth time, I have to admit to feeling unusually nervous. Rose is due to arrive at any second and I have no idea how this evening is going to pan out. Thanks to the staff I employ, the house itself is looking sparkling clean. A sixteenth century, eight bedroom manor house, I can't deny I live in an amazing home although in all honesty, it is ridiculously large for one person. I find myself shutting up a significant proportion of the rooms, only managing to put them to use when I host a large party.

One of the main aspects I'm worried about tonight is the food which I've prepared from scratch myself. Although, given Rose's own culinary abilities, I'm guessing she'll be pretty impressed with the beef wellington that is currently cooking in the oven. I smile in memory of her the state of her kitchen the previous night, smoke billowing profusely from the oven. My amusement is quickly stifled when I ponder the second aspect that currently concerns me. Will Rose be impressed with me?

So far, on the two occasions we've met, I've kind of been responsible for rescuing her in some way, and she has undoubtedly felt grateful as a result. The first time was when she fell, the second time, when I identified her stalker. But tonight, she is just going to get plain old James. Is that going to be enough, I wonder? My ruminations are cut short by the doorbell. Taking a sharp inhale, I smooth back my hair and stride towards the front door, briefly glancing at my reflection in the mirror en route. Only one way to find out...

As the door swings open, I am temporarily lost for words. There, standing on the doorstep of my home, is Rose. She looks completely gorgeous. Dressed in a thick winter coat, her colt-like legs exposed to the elements from just below the knee, she is good enough to eat. My eyes rove to her long, blonde hair, which is piled perfectly upon her head, before landing on her exquisite, smiling face. I've always privately scorned those who believe in love at first sight, but now, I have to admit I'm becoming far less certain in my forthright opinions.

'Come in,' I murmur, temporarily lost for any intelligent conversation. Stepping back, I allow her inside. Pausing in the hallway, she shyly unbuttons her coat, to uncover a short, black lacy dress. Unable to prevent myself, I step forwards and help her to unwrap. She's just like a Christmas present, which I can't wait to explore.

'Oh! James,' she groans, her eyes fluttering closed as my hands slide around the curve of her waist.

It all happens so fast. Within a heartbeat, we find ourselves returned to the equivalent intensity of the previous night. Fingers, mouths, hands, lips, arms, tongues, teeth; all are employed in a bid to get as close as physically possible. We are both breathing heavily when the kitchen timer starts to beep piercingly. Naturally, I back away slightly, staring into her sparkling, lust-laden eyes.

'I need to go and save our dinner,' I growl, my voice barely capable of operating.

'Okay,' she gasps, clearly shaken.

It takes all of my willpower to release her from my intimate hold. With a reassuring smile, I collect her coat from the floor where it landed some time previously and hang it up, en route to the kitchen. By the time I've pulled the beef wellington out of the oven to rest, she has joined me.

'You have a seriously beautiful home,' she states in admiration. 'Amazing...'

'Thank you,' I reply, with a small bow of my head. 'Dinner is ready, but let me know if it's too early for you?' I don't typically eat until later and the beef wellington can be eaten cold if necessary. I only suggested Rose arrive at half past six, in order to get her here as early as physically possible.

'I'm not very hungry,' she admits, cheeks still flushed from the excitement of our recent kiss.

'So, what are you, then?' I enquire in a teasing tone.

She gazes at me thoughtfully, as though weighing up whether she dares to share what is on her mind.

'Go on,' I encourage.

'Horny.'

For the longest time, I watch her, my head tilted slightly to one side, the air between us crackling with static electricity.

'And what *exactly* do you expect me to do about that?' I murmur seductively. My cock, which was already throbbing from our earlier kiss, twitches back into life, particularly when she rolls her lower lip gently between her teeth.

'Well,' Rose replies hopefully. 'This is our third date.'

'This is our *second* date,' I correct, walking slowly towards her, until only the kitchen island separates us. Sliding my hand forwards, I intertwine my fingers with hers and am gratified to hear a low moan echoing from Rose's throat, the instant we touch. 'Surely you aren't counting the night I carried you home as a date, are you?'

'To be honest, for the purposes of this conversation, I'll classify it any way necessary,' she admits, sounding increasingly desperate. 'Just so long as the evening ends with you inside me.'

'I'll tell you what,' I grunt, the image of my cock sliding into Rose's writhing body, temporarily overwhelming every other sense I possess. 'I'll compromise. Tonight can be all about your pleasure. But sex still doesn't happen until we've enjoyed our third date.'

'That doesn't sound very fair on you,' replies Rose, failing to hide just how much the thought of what I'm offering turns her on.

'Believe me, experiencing your pleasure will give me the biggest thrill possible,' I admit. And I mean it too. 'Follow me.'

Taking her lightly by the hand, I lead the way, guiding her upstairs and into my bedroom. Abandoning her in the centre of my room beside the bed, I dim the lights and draw the curtains. From a distance, I take a moment to gaze in admiration; she is exquisite, standing there in her short black dress and heels, arms hanging by her sides, trembling slightly as she trustingly observes me.

Slowly, I approach and kneel before her. Running my hand down her shapely calf, she uses my shoulder to retain her balance, as I remove first one, then the other shoe. Remaining where I am, my hands run up the backs of her legs, enjoying the sensation of her sheer stockings. When I reach her exposed upper thigh, she inhales swiftly, as my fingers circle in an investigative way, occasionally nudging the edge of her panties.

'Lay down for me,' I request, over her light moans. I can already sense her legs trembling violently as I teasingly explore. She seems far from stable and I don't want Rose to lose her balance.

With a powerful blast of exhilaration, I acknowledge that Rose is in my home, on my bed, desperately awaiting my touch. That is quite a heady combination by anyone's standards. Reaching up to stroke a strand of hair away from her face, my fingers gradually make their way towards her mouth. Immediately, her lips open as she attempts to pull one of my fingers inside. I swallow hard, unsure whether I can truly deliver what I've promised. Once Rose is in the throes of orgasm, will I seriously have the willpower to not simply bury myself inside her contorting body and drive her onwards?

Replacing my fingers with my mouth, I kiss her deeply, passionately, leaving no doubt as to the intensity of my affections. But how should I progress? No-one could deny that she's feeling seriously horny, but should I use that to my advantage and tease her, making her beg for her release? Leave her quivering for the longest time, as I deny her for my own pleasure? I hope she doesn't assume that just because I'm well brought up and monied, I'm vanilla in bed. Perhaps she'll be happy to find out that I'm not…

Moving to straddle her, I break our kiss, nipping randomly down her neck, generating shrieks of surprise that simply encourage me to continue. I quickly ascertain her dress has a hidden zip that starts under her arm and runs down the length of her torso. As my hand migrates to the appropriate location and starts to slowly open the zip, exposing her warm skin to the air, so my mouth migrates to somewhere far more exciting. Unconcerned that her dress still covers her breasts, I hover over her chest, before placing my teeth carefully around the outline of one delicate nipple. Then slowly, I increase the pressure, until the tender flesh is firmly clamped.

'Urrggghhhhhh,' groans Rose, emitting a low guttural noise that makes me throb even harder and confirms that I've hit the exact spot I was aiming for.

Continuing to hold her securely, having dealt with the zip, my hand slides beneath her dress, teasingly running my fingers over her sensitive tummy and making her twist and spasm beneath my control.

'Fuuu-uuuck!' she cries into the otherwise still, quiet air of my room. Her tone echoes the desperation that I feel, making me evermore determined to give this incredible woman the night of her life.

Swiftly, I release her from my mouth, but only for as long as it takes for me to drag her dress down to her hips. Within seconds, my mouth has returned to her other nipple, this time trapping it through her black lace bra. Unable to deal with the pleasure I'm flooding her with, she tries to grab at my shoulders, fingernails digging in deep through my shirt. With a grunt, I retract slightly, encircling her wrists in my much larger hands and pinning her firmly to the bed.

'Are you sure you want this?' I demand. It's important to be certain; I have a feeling that once I properly start, I'll have serious difficulty stopping until she doesn't have a single orgasm left to offer me.

'I'm sure,' she gasps, swallowing hard. 'God, yes.'

In that case, let the games commence.

CHAPTER 8

ROSE

Jesus Christ. James has barely touched me and already I'm a gibbering, trembling puddle of arousal, willing to sign up to anything and everything he's offering. Right now, his tongue is making its way across my heaving chest, leaving a trail of searing passion in its wake. Reacting instinctively, my back arches in order to thrust my nipples further towards him, desperately pleading for him to demonstrate some form of mercy. I need to feel him... properly, but frustratingly, the majority of my clothing remains firmly in place.

My body rolls and contracts violently, as his teasing fingers gradually head across the soft skin on my tummy. I'm panting heavily, my throat unnaturally dry. A long moan escapes me when his mouth drifts further down, tongue slipping along the waistband of my panties. As my head rolls from side to side, eyes flickering closed, I'm aware of his fingers grasping the material of my dress which is still rucked up around my hips. The feel of the garment being dragged slowly down my legs and away, causes a great rush of relief to flood me. At last, he's going to attend to my increasingly urgent desire to orgasm.

Unbelievably, although I continue to gasp, it is due to frustration, not ecstasy, as his undoubtedly purposeful teasing continues. My nipples feel unnaturally tight, my pussy throbbing with each and every beat of my heart and yet, no relief follows. His fingers trail all over me, yet never where I want them to land. It's the same with his mouth as it slides delicately across my trembling skin.

'Pleeeee-aaase.' The fraught cry escapes my mouth before I'm even aware of speaking, hips rolling wantonly in an attempt to gain even the slightest contact. I'm aware of James's slightly stubbly chin grazing me, which only increases the overwhelming sensation of our joint lust.

I make the mistake of gazing deeply into his eyes and automatically, I am dumbstruck. Without breaking our connection, he shuffles down the bed, pushing my legs wide open and causing me to gasp dramatically. Immediately, my internal muscles clamp down hard. I observe an extremely wicked grin slowly spreading across his face, as he lowers himself down. His actions elicit a whimper from me which swiftly conjure up images of hot, sweaty sex and devilish acts of pleasure.

The feel of James's warm, moist mouth being dragged along my inner thigh, adjacent to the seam of my panties, is practically unbearable. Blasted with an excess of anticipation, I am forced to bite my lip in an effort to maintain control, my resultant squeal of frustration echoing across the room. I observe the corners of his eyes crinkle, suggesting the bastard is amused at the insane state to which I'm being driven. And then, he readjusts slightly, and all my thoughts dissolve; my only focus is on this man and when, how or even if he will consent to touch me.

With a carnal growl, James inhales deeply. He is hovering centimetres above my wide-open pussy now. It is protected only by the thinnest layer of silk, which separates me from the blissful indulgence of his touch. My swollen, wet clit throbs vigorously; a sensation only set to increase when James nudges his nose against my panties, disturbing my slippery, over-delicate flesh beneath.

'Please, please,' I chant, no longer capable of logical thought. Desire has invaded all aspects of my body and mind. Only one thing exists right now; this man, in this moment. Nothing else matters.

I'm aware of arousal seeping through my underwear; a condition magnified when James dares to lick them from the outside. He is tasting me, without providing any of the anticipated pleasure which such an act should naturally supply. His tongue occasionally threatens to slide beneath the flimsy barrier, but never does so. It's unbearable. No, worse than that. It's excruciating! To know that so much unharnessed pleasure is being prohibited by a small scrap of material. All the talent I already know James possesses in the tip of his tongue and playful fingers, thanks to the kisses we've shared. Even worse, from the tone of his low groans, he seems to be finding his own perverse form of pleasure in leading me right up to the very edge of euphoria, happy to leave me dangling over the void. For there is no doubt that he knows exactly what effect his torturous actions are having on me. No doubt at all.

'Oh God, please...' I gasp in utter desperation. James must have recognised something in my tone and decided to be merciful. With his mouth remaining in position, he reaches up and slides one hand beneath my back, unclipping and removing my bra with practiced ease. Without thinking, my soft hands automatically capture my breasts, kneading gently, before squeezing my hard nipples, in the hope of providing even the slightest relief. I wouldn't normally act so provocatively, but James has built me up into such a frenzy of desperation that I will do just about anything to lessen this burning hunger inside.

'Fuck, you're *so* sexy,' he grunts, enjoying the floor show I am unexpectedly providing.

Immediately, he returns his mouth to my panties, this time dragging his teeth straight up the centre. With a yowl of despair, my hips twist urgently as the unusual sensation causes a pulse of electricity to sizzle across my clit. Every noisy breath I vent is simply further proof of my struggle to maintain even the smallest semblance of self-control. And then, at last, it happens. James teasingly wiggles his fingers beneath the waistband of my panties, zig-zagging them slowly down my thighs and away, leaving me naked, except for my stockings. My legs are pushed wide open once more, placing me in an unbearably vulnerable position. I am completely exposed to him; he has the access and ability to do whatever he wants to me right now. Yet, instead of feeling anxious about all the power he holds, I'm surprised to feel primed, sensual and above all, safe.

'I'm keeping these,' James growls lustfully. Scrunching my panties into his large hand, he lifts the garment to his face and inhales deeply. His actions cause my eyes to open wide in shock; I had no idea he would be like this. Although, please don't get me wrong...I'm beyond thrilled that he is.

With breathtaking tenderness, James dips into the wet pool he is responsible for creating, holding on tight as my body crumbles around him. After the agonising build-up of desire I've been forced to endure, his touch is constant and sure. Even to my ears, my moans sound low, continuous and almost melodic as he skilfully intensifies my pleasure until the outcome of our coupling becomes utterly predictable.

Thanks to James combining his probing tongue with a glorious pressure placed around my clit by his continually stroking fingers, I rapidly ascend towards what I don't realise at the time will be the first of many orgasms over the next few hours. As my skin becomes increasingly flushed, I start to gasp in a staccato fashion, my muscles tightening more intensely with every second that passes. And then it happens; an explosion of pleasure, joy and sheer relief as I come hard, grinding down against him.

Afterwards, I literally can't move. It is all I can do, to continue heaving oxygen into my gasping lungs. The first sensation I'm truly aware of is just how wet I am. My pussy feels swollen beyond belief and a wave of embarrassment threatens to take hold, simply because of the state I've got myself into. James, on the other hand, seems to be relishing it. With a satisfied growl, he visibly savours my arousal, before starting a slow migratory route northwards. Kissing appreciatively up my torso, he takes his sweet time to suckle on my nipples, almost sending me straight back over the edge once more. When our mouths finally meet, his tongue claims mine, completely and unconditionally, the taste of my own pleasure on his delectable lips.

'That was incredible,' I sigh, when we eventually come up for air.

'Mmmmm,' he agrees, a satiated smile spreading across his face. 'But please don't think I'm anywhere near finished with you yet.'

And James wasn't joking. For the longest time, I am held captive in his bedroom, a prisoner of my own lust. Dizzy and utterly replete, I am eventually released to make my unsteady way down the stairs. Holding onto the bannister with one hand and James with the other, I gratefully drop onto a bar stool in the kitchen. James flits around the kitchen preparing our dinner, which incidentally my growling stomach is now desperate for, after such a marathon workout. I can't help but admire him, perhaps feeling a little awe-struck. I have never known anything like the pleasure my body has been exposed to this evening. And, as promised, the entire time we spent upstairs was dedicated to me. Just me. James remained fully clothed throughout, gently but firmly pushing my hands away, whenever they dared to wander too far.

'Do you want to sit here to eat?' he asks, suddenly breaking my pleasurable daydream. 'Or in the lounge?'

'Whatever you prefer,' I sigh. I feel so spaced-out and happy that, quite honestly, very little matters to me right now. James obviously notices the change in my demeanour. Leaning sexily over me, his hands start to crawl up my thighs, edging my legs apart. All of a sudden, I'm hyperalert once more, addictively awaiting his further touch. You see, as per his request, my panties remain in his possession. Consequently, I am naked beneath my dress, providing him with the freedom to take control of me whenever and however he pleases.

CHAPTER 9

JAMES

Okay. So I'm officially captivated. Rose is, quite simply, the most amazing woman I have ever met. And spending those first few hours discovering exactly what turns her on, while experiencing the overwhelming joy of her coming around my fingers and tongue; well, I don't even have any words for that.

Despite the underlying sexual current which continuously sparks between us, we do manage to enjoy a late but pleasant supper together, along with a good bottle of wine. For my own amusement, I have made us both a hot chocolate to round our meal off, topped with whipped cream and chocolate sprinkles. The instant I hand the beverage across to her, she stares at me challengingly. I simply flash my eyebrows back in amusement, enjoying the playful relationship we are starting to build.

I'm not sure if she's doing it on purpose, but I'm finding Rose to be increasingly tactile; a hand accidentally-on-purpose nudging my thigh, reaching out for my chest, brushing a crumb from my lips. It soon becomes clear that her actions are being made very much on purpose, when she readjusts her seating position, opening her legs slightly to ensure I get a full view up her short dress. Pink, glistening and swollen, she is clearly still incredibly turned on.

'Stop teasing me,' I growl. I intend to stand by my three date rule but, in all seriousness, Rose is testing me to my very limits right now. I'm counting down the seconds until our third date; boy, is she going to be in some trouble.

'Or else, what?' she asks. Buoyed with confidence that I intend to stand by my promise, she is clearly intent on getting a little payback for the prolonged teasing she was made to endure upstairs. 'What you gonna do about it?'

With a growl, I clamp down my jaw, determined not to reciprocate. Switching on the television, I collect our empty mugs and disappear into the kitchen. I'm as hard as hell, but I know that isn't going to change tonight. The highly edible Rose is practically making it her purpose in life to ensure I am set to suffer. Pulling down my shirt to hide the worst of the evidence, I make my way back to the lounge. Taking my place beside her, I pull her into a gentle embrace. The moment she snuggles up against my chest, I have an incredible realisation; this is *exactly* where I'm supposed to be, and with whom.

For a while, we simply relax, our bodies closely embracing, both highly aware of each other but doing nothing to further the situation. There is something on the television in the background, but to be honest, I'm completely oblivious to it. All of my attention is solely on Rose. I'm doing pretty well keeping my hands to myself, given I know her panties are safely tucked under my pillow upstairs, but I am guilty of stroking the nape of her neck. My actions are producing a low moan in her throat, each time she breathes which, in turn, has made me harder still.

Somewhere in the distance, the grandfather clock strikes. My eyes drift towards the clock on the mantelpiece, astonished to discover that it's midnight. Knowing I hold the most amazing woman in my arms, I still feel unexpectedly disappointed. For all the best reasons, time has raced away from us this evening and it's getting late. How long before she makes her excuses and leaves me?

'It's midnight,' Rose observes. Here it comes. A polite but firm excuse.

'It is,' I agree, trying to sound upbeat.

'You know what that means?'

'No.' I can't prevent myself from smiling at the mischievous glint in her eye.

'It's a new day. We can officially count this moment onwards as our third date.'

A knot of excitement takes hold of my abdomen; a throbbing heat, a shot of adrenaline. It feels as though my body is awakening, preparing, readying, although for what, I'm not exactly sure.

'Meaning?' I growl, as she wriggles out of my embrace to kneel on the carpet between my knees.

'Meaning, I literally can't wait another second longer,' she sighs.

As she gazes up at me, I register a note of uncertainty, as though she's silently asking permission for what she longs to do. My eyes open a little wider, my jaw a little slacker, as her delicate fingers move to the button fly of my jeans. Groaning submissively, my eyes flutter closed, before quickly snapping back open; I don't want to miss a single second of this. With a smile, she exposes the black jockey shorts I'm wearing, my thick length instantly obvious. Using a single fingertip, she follows the outline from my swollen head, pooling with pre-cum, all the way down the shaft. Her actions elicit a long, low moan from my throat, while I twitch continuously under her intimate supervision.

When Rose attempts to push what I'm wearing, I eagerly assist, my cock springing up to meet her, the instant it is released from the confines of clothing.

'Mmmmmm,' she sighs pleasurably, as her warm, soft hand wraps around my girth, stroking tenderly.

'Oh Jeez...' I grunt. My chest is working hard, accepting long, deep breaths of air, and still I feel lightheaded.

In disbelief, I watch as she circles her tongue over my throbbing flesh, growing in confidence with every stroke. From her fluttering eyelids and thrilling moans, it is clear she is relishing the taste of me. Increasingly, I'm aware of my eyes losing focus, as she slowly feeds my cock further into her enthusiastic mouth, her hand working in perfect synchronisation, taking ownership. An unexpected warmth floods my chest; there is no denying that I desire this woman with every fibre of my being.

'You moaning while your mouth is sucking my cock, is such a turn on,' I admit, my voice sounding little more than a low rumble. Instinctively, my hands reach for her head, stroking her hair, gently assisting with the rhythm.

Very soon, I'm aware of Rose groaning enthusiastically as my cock starts to weep pre-cum. It's such an incredibly sexy thought to know she is savouring the taste of me, just as I readily consumed her earlier. But there is only so much my body is able to withstand and I'm near to reaching my limits. Ordinarily, I'd have no qualms about allowing her naughty teasing to reach its natural end, but the very first time I come, I should be deep inside Rose, ensuring she feels equally as amazing as I do.

'You're gonna have to stop,' I just about manage to utter, even though it goes against every physical desire I possess. 'You're gonna make me come.'

'Mmmmm,' Rose groans, showing absolutely no sign that she wishes to comply with my request. As my heart rate increases, hips gently rocking in time with the breathtaking rhythm she has set up, I feel myself weaken. Perhaps I should just go with it and submit to exploding down the back of her throat. But then, as a light tingling sensation threatens to take hold in my balls, something inside me snaps and I roar like a wounded animal. Rose immediately retracts in surprise, giving me the chance to scoop her into my arms and carry her straight back upstairs, my cock aching and spasming with every step I take.

Throwing her onto my bed, I rip away the rest of my clothes, as she watches with uncontained delight.

'Your turn,' I demand, with a nod in her direction. Thrillingly, she accepts my command, slipping out of her dress to squirm naked beneath me. Meanwhile, I grab a condom from a nearby drawer, ripping the packet open with my teeth and rolling it on in record time.

'You know you've been asking for this all evening, don't you?' I growl against her ear, as I position myself, pushing her thighs wide apart.

'Yes,' she shudders, her body language confirming that she wants this equally as much as I do.

'I'm gonna fuck you now. Hard,' I moan, swiping the head of my cock through her wetness, only to create the sweetest breathy murmur I have ever heard. 'But the last thing I want to do is hurt you...just say stop if you need me to...'

And with that, I start to inch my way forwards. I have every intention of fucking this woman into the middle of next week, but I'm not so much of a bastard that I'm not going to start off gently. I fully appreciate she needs to get used to the fullness of my girth, before I can really give her my all.

For some time, the air between us is filled with breathy cries, gasps and moans, as we luxuriate in the incredible feeling of our bodies melding into one. Interspersed with deep, sensual kisses, we both revel in the intensity of the pleasure we're creating.

'Ready?' I whisper at last, nipping up Rose's neck and across to her mouth. She doesn't answer with words, but the fingernails in my back and increased compression around my cock informs me that her answer is yes. Having taken possession of her mouth with my own, I move my hips with increasing speed and power, my aching balls starting to slap resoundingly against her ass.

I know I must hold it together, but it's nigh on impossible. Rose is seconds away from orgasm, writhing out of control beneath me. I can feel the phenomenal force of her pleasure intensifying, just before she screams out my name.

'Go on, baby,' I encourage, but her pussy is spasming so hard around my cock, I can hardly bear to continue. Each thrust is a monumental effort of self-control, knowing the sensations my actions will invoke. With a growl of despair, I keep going, fucking my way through each of her orgasms, indulging Rose in her prolonged pleasure. My mind is a swirl of thoughts as I suppress my own yearning to come and instead move onto auto-pilot. There is one thing I know for sure, however; I will never forget this night. Neither of us will.

CHAPTER 10

ROSE

James has obliterated all preconceived ideas I ever had about sex; I never, ever knew it could be like this. He manages to shift seamlessly between rampant, dirty fucking to something decidedly more tender, as the mood takes him. And nothing is outside the limits; every position explored, every wicked fantasy shared. Apparently, in bed, this man has no boundaries.

Having taken possession of my entire being some time previously, mentally I feel as though I'm riding a chemically-induced high. Apparently only currently capable of producing a sound set mid-way between a sob of despair and cry of utter pleasure, I can't put into words how James is making me feel. I just know that I never want this experience to end.

Having said that, I can feel myself starting to tire. I guess that's inevitable, when you've been brought to orgasm as many times as I have today. And yet I still find the energy to keep rocking back against his thick, rigid cock. Right now, James is behind me, his hands firmly holding my hips, pulling my body back against him to increase the intensity as he thrusts forwards. I can feel the arousal streaming down the inside of my thighs, wetter than I have ever known. We are both moaning long and low. It simply feels too goddamn good to stop.

'Roll onto your back for me,' he murmurs, tenderly pulling out and assisting me over. He's done this a lot; breaking the rhythm at the point he's getting close to coming. It has meant our games have gone on for a long, long time, but he must be seriously desperate by now.

Hungrily we gaze at each other, eyes locked together, as James immediately drives himself back inside. I bite my lower lip, legs gripping around his back, as I silently encourage him onwards. This change in position is resulting in a different part of me being stimulated, a new way for James to turn me on. I'm so wet, so swollen; I've never reacted this intensely in my life. If I can walk at all tomorrow, it will be a miracle, but right now, that doesn't concern me. All that matters is happening right here, right now.

James uses one of his hands to stroke my face, as he peppers my mouth with kisses. I can't help but reciprocate, revelling in the touch of his skin, as my hands stroke his muscled back and incredible ass. And all the while, he continues to rhythmically grind against me, responsible for providing so much pleasure. The sex has changed to become very slow, tantalisingly seductive and breathtakingly intense. If I ever had any doubt as to what we are doing, I don't now. We are making love. Pure and simple.

I watch James's eyes flutter closed as a low growl escapes his throat. I know he's trying to maintain control over himself, but I don't want that any more. I want to feel the rush of excitement, as he loses complete control inside my satiated body and allows me to witness him at his most defenceless.

'Come for me,' I murmur, reaching up to stroke the hair from his damp forehead as we share a small smile. 'Please.'

Automatically, his mouth finds mine, our lips clashing together with unexpected urgency. Immediately, instinct informs me that my command is going to be followed; James has at last mentally given himself permission to come. With his entire weight securing me between him and the mattress, James reaches for my wrists, raising them above my head. I am trapped. Despite my exhaustion, I utter a deep groan of submission, my internal muscles automatically clamping hard around his cock as he continues to thrust inside. I've orgasmed so many times, I honestly thought I was done for the night, but now I'm not so sure.

Rising up slightly, James flashes me a cheeky glance, before his mouth drops to my left nipple, encompassing it with his teeth and clamping down gently.

'Oohhhhhhhh!' I squeal, my tired body suddenly wide awake and shaking with urgent need. 'Oh! You can't!'

'Mmmmm,' grins James, momentarily releasing me to provide focus on my other side. 'I *absolutely* can.'

I'm astonished to realise that an orgasm is slowly starting to approach; like a train running from some distance along the line. It may well take a little time to reach me, but there is a certain degree of inevitability. Reach me it will.

'You're gonna come for me first, Rose,' murmurs James, as his mouth finds my neck once more. It's one of the many hotspots that James had delighted in discovering tonight, and then exploited for his own wicked pleasure.

'Oh God!' I gasp, knowing he speaks the truth. The sensations have started to build inside me as I tighten still further around him; a warmth, a pressure, a need to release, an urgency to submit to my most basic need. I close my eyes, head rolling back into the pillow, starting to groan with every powerful thrust James makes.

I sense a change in his demeanour. A low moan tells me he's close. His thrusts are becoming longer and deeper, his cock swelling noticeably inside of me, as he prepares to reach the very deepest parts of my body and soul.

'Fuck!' I yelp. Whatever he's doing is working. Oh God. I'm so close. So damn close. But I am exhausted. I need more. 'Fuck me!' I urge him. If he really needs me to come, then I need him hard, frenzied and uncontrolled.

Probably because he knows there is precious little time left, James reacts swiftly. Lifting one of my legs towards his shoulder, he ploughs straight back inside, hammering me for all he's worth.

'Oh fuck!' he cries out. Clamping around him with every

remaining ounce of strength I possess, I submit to the impressive power of my climax.

Riding the waves of pleasure, I'm aware of very little, except James working hard at maximising my gratification for as long as physically possible. But eventually, he must succumb. With a groan of pleasure subtly laced with surrender, he powers one final time inside and ejaculates with impressive force. It immediately sets off a further flurry of reactions inside me, driving him on.

Gradually, our movements slow and I feel myself descending from the most incredible high. I barely have the energy to remain present, but I can feel James very carefully withdrawing from my pulsing, quenched yet shattered body.

'Stay the night with me?' he groans, dropping a kiss on my nose as he gathers me into his arms.

'Mmmmmm.' That's the only response I'm capable of. But I do stay the night with him. For that night, and every night which follows.

EPILOGUE

ROSE

Six months have passed since James and I first met and life is good. No, scratch that. I'm blessed to be able to call James my boyfriend and life is *amazing*. For a start, my nuisance phone calls are a thing of the past. Not only did they stop dead, after my first meal out with James in the pub, but Ben the would-be stalker is completely out of the picture. According to village gossip, he started up his antics with another unsuspecting target and his wife found out and left him. They had to sell their house and have since both moved away from the area.

My dear, faithful Henry is almost as content as I am. Given we spend a significant proportion of our time at James's home these days, Henry suddenly has a five acre, rabbit-filled garden to disappear into whenever he wishes, plus hundreds of acres of estate land beyond that. And of course, the icing on the cake is that their gamekeeper doesn't dare enter into a shouting match with me anymore, when Henry accidentally chases one of the deer...which he invariably does on a far too regular basis.

Sitting in front of James's dressing table, I thoughtfully start to brush my hair. Reflected in the mirror, I can my possessions peppering the room; clothing, makeup, magazines, handbag, dog sprawled across the rug at the base of the bed... I'd love to live with James permanently, but I haven't raised the subject yet, just in case he feels it's too soon. That doesn't stop me appreciating that James has been systematically making every aspect of my life better, since the very first day we met.

My daydream is broken when I become aware of the man himself entering the bedroom. With a towel slung low around his hips, his remarkable body still slightly damp from the shower, he looks good enough to eat. I glance at the clock, wondering if I have time to do just that.

'And we're *sure* tonight is a good idea, are we?' James asks. He's attempting to be serious, but both his tone and his expression are giving him away.

We've invited Mary over for dinner, along with one of James's best mates, Thomas. It isn't a blind date, as such. Mary and Thomas met for the first time at a barbeque we hosted last weekend and they got along like the proverbial house on fire. I'm just hoping to fan the flames a little more. I can't imagine anything better than my best friend finding the intense happiness I'm enjoying right now with James. There is simply nothing to compare.

'It's a fantastic idea and you know it!' England is wallowing in a mini-heatwave at present, so we have plans to eat outside. What could be more romantic than a balmy, candlelit evening meal under the stars? My matchmaking plan is almost guaranteed to succeed!

'Hmmmm, if you say so,' he growls, not sounding overly convinced. 'You don't think we're being a bit too obvious? They won't feel uncomfortable with the focus so clearly being on the two of them?'

'No...' Silently I concede that he might have a point.

'I mean, if it were a celebration dinner...' he suggested. 'That would allow everyone to be a little more relaxed?'

'Celebration?' I can see my face screwed up with confusion in the mirror, as James approaches me from behind.

'Yeah,' he says, softly stroking my shoulders and sending all manner of delicious sensations through me. 'Say, for example, if you were to agree to move in with me...'

Gasping, I spin around in my seat to face him head on.

'Seriously?' He doesn't need to reply with words. The enormous smile on his face says it all. 'Are you only asking me, to save your friend from suffering any discomfort tonight?' I joke, tenderly stroking my fingers across the palm of his hand.

'Damn! You've seen straight through my plan!' he chuckles, placing an open-mouthed kiss along the sensitive skin on the inside of my wrist. 'Although, on second thoughts, maybe we should just leave things as they are? If you move in with me, I'll be forced to find a new tenant for your house.'

'I knew it!' I exclaim, pulling away the lone towel from his hips and attempting to slap his perfect ass, in retaliation for attempting to mislead me all those months ago. He is my landlord after all!

'Don't worry,' he smirks, capturing my hands and pulling me over to the bed. Giggling, we fall upon it, a tangle of limbs, as he makes an admirable attempt to tug away my clothing. 'I've got a really good idea about how you can earn back your security deposit.'

THE END

Check out other books by Fenella at www.fenellaashworth.com

THANK YOU

Thank you for reading this book.

Please do consider leaving a review, which is an enormous help to self-published authors such as myself as it helps us to compete with the big publishing companies! I've written plenty of steamy romances so please take a look at the book list if you're short of ideas for your next read.

Website: www.fenellaashworth.com
Newsletter: eepurl.com/gKH2OL

WHAT TO READ NEXT?

Need inspiration on what to read next? There are a number of 'Black Lace and Promises' story collections by Fenella Ashworth, all available from Amazon. The fourth book contains the following stories:

SEVEN WISHES - Sexy racing driver Bradley Drake seems to have it all; ample money, sleek cars, public adoration and a beautiful actress on his arm. That is until a car accident crushes his body along with his dreams.

In comparison, with her beaten-up old van and boringly normal life, Clara Collins is proud to be ordinary. Exceptional at her job as a live-in nurse, it isn't long before Clara proves that she is unlike any other woman Brad has ever met.

On paper, they are two people who couldn't be more different. But when exceptional circumstances bring them together, could Brad and Clara discover what they were each missing, within the other?

. . .

OUR TIME - ANNIE gets the shock of her life when her son's new Geography teacher turns out to be none other than her own high school crush from twenty years ago. Despite their obvious attraction, Annie and Jack failed to get together back then. But can this chance meeting reignite the secret flame which still burns so strongly between them?

APOLOGY NOT ACCEPTED - Carrie is a strong-willed, independent woman who isn't afraid to stand up for herself; character traits which occasionally get her into trouble. Following a misunderstanding with the delectable Richard, she finds herself needing to offer up an apology. To her astonishment, it's an apology that, for his own wicked reasons, Richard refuses to accept. But it doesn't take long for their intensely strong attraction to override any initial playful animosity, and that's when the fireworks really begin.

ABOUT THE AUTHOR

Fenella is the author of many a steamy romance.

She lives in the South of England where her time is divided equally between looking after her family, drinking wine, turning her smutty thoughts into stories, and (possibly most importantly of all), avoiding doing any housework.

Much of Fenella's inspiration appears during peaceful, early morning walks with her mentally deranged Spaniel. Consequently, she spends her time bumbling around the countryside deep in thought, falling into rabbit holes while remaining completely oblivious to the most spectacular sunrises.

www.fenellaashworth.com

Printed in Great Britain
by Amazon